The Crimes of Middlemoor Estate

J. R. Beeton

Copyright 2025 J.R. Beeton

The right of J.R. Beeton to be identified as the Author of the Work has been asserted by her in accordance with the Copyright, Designs and Patents Act 1988.

First published in 2025
Print ISBN 978-1-0369-1185-0

Apart from any use permitted under UK copyright law, this publication may only be reproduced, stored, or transmitted, in any form, or by any means, with prior permission, in accordance with the terms of licences issued by the Copyright Licensing Agency.

All characters in this publication are fictitious and any resemblance to real persons, living or dead, is purely coincidental.

Dedication

This book is dedicated to the loving memory of CM, Little B, Myles, RK, and Baby B. Your spirits continue to inspire and guide us every day, and your memories are deeply cherished in our hearts.

In their honour, I will sign twenty-five copies of this book. These special editions hold unique significance, symbolising the love and remembrance of our dear ones who left us too soon. All proceeds from the sale of the signed copies will be donated to SANDS, a charity devoted to supporting families affected by the loss of a baby.

This charity provides invaluable resources and a compassionate community for those navigating the difficult journey of grief and recovery. By purchasing this book, you are not only keeping the memories of CM, Little B, Myles, RK, and Baby B alive but also contributing to a cause that brings so much comfort to countless families.

Your support will help SANDS continue their vital work, offering solace and guidance to those in need. Thank you for joining this effort to honour the memory of these special babies and for helping make a difference in the lives of many others.

TAVISTOCK HERITAGE & HILLS

Picturesque Village of Middlemoor Holds Secrets Behind its Stately Charm

Nestled in the idyllic south-west of England, Middlemoor village in Devon exudes a timeless charm, with its close-knit community and sweeping landscapes just three miles from the Cornish border. On any given summer day, the village hums with familiar faces, including the local eccentric in his trademark shorts, boat shoes, and bright yellow socks, leisurely greeting passers-by with the warmth only small-village life can offer. But is everything in Middlemoor as it seems?

Beyond the village centre, Middlemoor Estate stands as a testament to the area's historic grandeur. The sprawling estate, anchored by a majestic 17th-century mansion, has been the ancestral home of the Ashworth family since the early 1600s. Currently, Mr. Henry Magnus Ashworth presides over the estate alongside his wife, Julianna Elisabeth, and their son, Benedict George. They share their home with a loyal companion, Duke the family dog, and a skilled team of estate staff who keep the historic residence running smoothly.

Sebastian Julius Archer, the dedicated estate manager, known affectionately as Seb, oversees every operation within the grand mansion, from coordinating staff duties to handling the Ashworth family's unique requests. Living in the mansion's east wing, Seb ensures Middlemoor Estate maintains its illustrious reputation.

One of the estate's cherished talents, Sally Clover, reigns over the kitchen as the resident chef. Known for her skill in creating lavish feasts, Sally keeps the Ashworth family and their staff well-nourished with locally sourced and exquisitely crafted meals. She resides in the gatehouse at the estate's main entrance with her husband, Terry, who serves as the head of security, vigilantly overseeing the estate's safety and its extensive CCTV network.

The estate's west wing houses Karin Johnston, Middlemoor's diligent housekeeper, who attends to every corner of the mansion with meticulous care, ensuring each room upholds the Ashworth family's impeccably high standards. Just a stone's throw away,

Danny Anderson, the estate's versatile gamekeeper, gardener, and all-round handyman, is stationed in the rear gatehouse. Known for his rugged charm and easy-going demeanour, Danny is a beloved fixture of the estate, even admired by his debonair colleague Seb.

Recent events have shown, however, that beneath Middlemoor Estate's polished surface, where every hedge is carefully trimmed and every corridor immaculately maintained, lies a story far more complex than meets the eye. What began as a picture-perfect portrayal of English aristocracy may reveal secrets long hidden, as whispers of deception and buried misdeeds grow louder within the village's rolling hills.

As Middlemoor stands on the brink of unveiling an unsavoury truth behind its stately walls, residents and visitors alike may find themselves rethinking the world behind this picturesque estate, wondering if they truly know the people they once trusted. The journey into Middlemoor's secrets appears to have just begun, promising an eye-opening look into the lives of those who seem to have it all. Will shadows of the past threaten to unravel it all?

Part One

Benedict

Chapter One

Early on the morning of Benedict's eighteenth birthday, Chef Sally, always an early riser, slipped out quietly to visit the local farmers market. The morning air was crisp, and the sun had just begun to rise, casting a golden glow over the stalls. Sally navigated through the bustling marketplace with practised ease. Her eyes eventually landed on the freshest strawberries available. The vendor greeted her with a smile, and he handed over a basket of plump ruby-red berries. Their sweet aroma promised a delightful addition to the day's special breakfast.

With her precious cargo secured, Sally made her way back to the house, the drive filled with thoughts of the secret pancake recipe passed down through generations. Each step in the recipe was a cherished ritual, from the precise mixing of the batter to the careful slicing of the strawberries. When she arrived back at Middlemoor Estate, she wasted no time and headed straight to the kitchen. She put on her apron, and her hands moved deftly as she began the preparations.

The rest of the household staff were a whirlwind of

activity. Seb and Karin coordinated the decorating efforts, ensuring every corner of the kitchen exuded festivity. Birthday banners with bold colourful letters were hung with care, and balloons in varying shades of blue and gold bobbed cheerfully as they were fastened in place. The room began to transform, reflecting the joy and excitement that Benedict's milestone birthday deserved.

Sally whisked the pancake batter, humming a soft tune as she worked. The scent of sizzling butter and cooking pancakes soon wafted through the air, mingling with the fragrance of fresh strawberries. She arranged the finished pancakes on a platter, artfully topping them with syrup and meticulously sliced strawberries, each piece placed with love and precision. The morning was more than a celebration; it was a tapestry of tradition, hard work, and the deep bond that held the family and staff together.

Benedict's alarm blared, cutting through the early morning silence. He groaned, stretched his arms, and reached over to silence the persistent buzz. Blinking away the remnants of sleep, he rolled out of bed and shuffled towards the en-suite bathroom. The cool tiled floor underfoot was a bracing wake-up call as he splashed water on his face, brushed his teeth, and combed his hair.

Once ready, he pulled on his favourite jeans and a comfortable T-shirt before stepping out into the hallway. The house was quiet. The soft morning light filtered through the curtains as he made his way down the long corridor. His footsteps echoed slightly in the spacious hall, adding to the tranquil atmosphere.

As he descended the grand main staircase, he could hear faint murmurs and rustling from the kitchen. Anticipation built within him: his family had something planned. When he pushed open the kitchen door, he was greeted by a lively scene.

Sebastian stood at the centre, gesturing dramatically with energy only he could muster at such an early hour. His extravagant birthday hat bounced with every movement, and he beamed when he spotted Ben.

"Oh, happy birthday, you wonderful, gorgeous boy!" Sebastian exclaimed, setting off a party popper that released a shower of colourful confetti.

Danny remained sitting at the table with his usual understated demeanour. He raised his mug of tea in a silent toast, a small smile playing on his lips. "Morning, birthday boy," he said, his voice a calming counterpoint to Sebastian's exuberance.

As Ben stepped into the kitchen, the rest of the staff joined in, popping party poppers in his direction. The room filled with the sound of laughter. Blushing from all the attention, Ben felt a rush of gratitude.

"Thanks, everyone," he said, his voice sincere as he looked at the cheerful faces around him. He took a seat at the table, the excitement and warmth of the moment making him feel deeply appreciated.

"Most welcome, Ben. Your celebratory breakfast is coming right up. What can I get you to drink? We have freshly brewed coffee, tea, home-made orange juice, or I can make you a cheeky Buck's Fizz?" asked Sally.

"Oooh, that's what I'm having. It's all about the

champers, darling!" said Seb, taking a large swig from his glass.

"A coffee would be grand, please, Sally. I need waking up. I didn't sleep too well last night," replied Ben.

Walking over with a coffee and his breakfast, Sally placed them in front of Ben. "Oh really? Any reason why?"

"Thank you, Sally. This looks amazing." Pausing, Ben licked his lips while adjusting his plate. "Just one of those nights. I subconsciously heard every little noise. I think I even heard Pa and Ma leave at one point." Ben took a mouthful of food.

"I did wonder if they had left already. The house seems rather quiet this morning, which is never possible with Mr. Ashworth about," joked Sally. Everyone began to dig into their breakfasts. "The car's still here. Do you know if they took a taxi, Terry?"

"I can only assume so. Mr. Ashworth asked if I could leave the front gates open all night. There's never any knowing with him. For all we know, he's probably gone in a chopper and that's why you kept waking up, Ben!" They all laughed in agreement.

"That's just reminded me," Terry said suddenly. "I'd better go close up the gates and get started on the CCTV tapes. It's changeover day, and that always takes a while, so I'll take my brekkie with me." He leaned over and kissed Sally on the head. "Thanks, love. Happy Birthday, bud." He ruffled Ben's hair before heading out.

"Before I forget, I found this by the front door," Sally said, handing over a sealed envelope addressed to Benedict. "I assume it's for you to open today."

Ben wiped syrup from his mouth, his curiosity piqued. He carefully opened the envelope and began to read the letter silently; the room was quiet as everyone watched his expression change from intrigue to surprise.

Dear Benedict,

Your mother and I deeply regret that we could not be with you this morning. However, as you understand, when duty calls, it is imperative for me to attend.

It is astonishing to think that eighteen years have passed since you entered our lives. How swiftly time flies! Witnessing your growth into an exceptional young man with ambitions akin to mine is truly marvellous. I have every confidence that you are prepared for this next step. Enclosed within this envelope, you will find the necessary paperwork. Kindly sign and forward them to our solicitors. Both your mother and I have completed our parts. The documents include the deeds to the house and full ownership of Ward & Ashworth. This tradition has been passed down through our family, and I received it from your grandfather, Warden, on my eighteenth birthday. How I miss that dear man! We are unsure of our exact return date, but rest assured, we will make it up to you, perhaps with a celebratory trip in honour of your eighteenth. I recall your fondness for Singapore.

With all our love, J and M x

Ben's eyes stared at the letter in disbelief. Could what he read truly be real? His gaze drifted away from the words on the page, searching for answers in the distance.

"What is it?" asked Karin.

"It's the deeds to the house and full ownership of the family business. I knew this day would come but I didn't expect it this early. An eighteenth birthday family tradition, apparently. First I've heard of it..."

"Hang on, does this mean you're the boss man now?" piped up Danny.

"Bloody hope not. You've all got no hope now." Ben chuckled.

"It's not that big of a responsibility when you have the best staff in the world. Presumably, you'll still have Keith overseeing the family business anyway?" Karin asked, her brow furrowed with concern.

"Absolutely. I'm not going to touch a thing. In fact, I'm just going to pretend I never saw this!" Ben laughed, quickly folding the documents and placing them back in the envelope.

They all laughed nervously with him.

After a long and awkward pause, Seb seized the moment. With a flourish, he pulled out an extravagantly wrapped gift from under the table and handed it to Ben, his eyes sparkling with excitement.

"Happy Birthday!" Seb excitedly squeaked.

"Aw, thanks, Seb." Ben tore open one side and pulled out a shirt that was most definitely not his style with its garish colours. Suppressing his initial shock, he forced a smile and thanked Seb again.

"It's Prada. Perhaps you can wear it tonight when you go for drinks with your friends." Seb's eyebrows rose with hope.

"Well, you'll certainly get some looks if that's what you're hoping for," Danny remarked, barely containing his laughter as he scrunched up his face. "It's the thought that counts, right?"

Seb's eyes widened in hurt, his mouth forming a perfect 'O'. Karin smacked Danny's arm and rolled her eyes.

"No, no, I love it. Thanks, Seb." Ben quickly pulled Seb into a hug, trying to mend the moment.

As they embraced, Ben's new responsibilities weighed down on him, even as he smiled at everyone around him.

Chapter Two

Sebastian walked into the kitchen and set his notebook and laptop down on the counter with a soft thud. He moved with deliberate grace as he poured himself a fresh coffee into his elegant Wedgwood Anthemion Blue teacup and placed it on its matching saucer. The rich aroma filled the room, adding to the cosy morning ambience.

As he glanced out of the kitchen window, he noticed Danny outside. Danny was carrying a ladder under his right arm and had a tool bag slung over his left shoulder. Sebastian watched with mild curiosity as he set up a workstation near the outdoor table and chairs. Raising an eyebrow and pursing his lips in bemusement, Sebastian made a mental note of Danny's position before strutting off to gather his things.

Returning moments later, Sebastian stepped onto the patio through the kitchen's back door. He was dressed in a thick winter coat, scarf, and gloves, but had complemented the look with stylish sunglasses. Balancing his notebook, laptop, and coffee, he carefully arranged himself at the outdoor table, exuding an air of purposeful nonchalance.

Danny glanced over, a mix of amusement and bewilderment crossing his face. He shook his head, a smile tugging at his lips, before turning back to his work. His task involved pinning plants to the wall, carefully positioning them to encourage their growth up the side of the house. Each movement was precise, his focus unwavering despite the curious-looking figure now seated nearby.

Sebastian sipped his coffee, savouring the flavour, then opened his laptop and notebook. The juxtaposition of his formal attire and the casual outdoor setting made for an amusing contrast, one that wasn't lost on either man as they settled into their respective tasks.

"Ahhh, it's rather a splendid morning." Seb took a deep breath while setting up his laptop.

"I think it's cold, and I'd much rather be working inside if I were doing computer work," said Danny, balancing on the ladder and using both hands to pin the wire. He pulled a face at Seb, knowing his true intentions for being outside in the cold.

Aware of Sebastian's attraction to him and despite Danny being very much a ladies' man, he couldn't resist the occasional playful flirt, enjoying the thrill of encouraging Sebastian a little. Sebastian, for his part, knew Danny wasn't interested in men, but that only fuelled his excitement; he loved the chase, finding joy in the tension between them.

Ben and Duke joined them on the patio. Ben was dressed in his running gear.

"Erm, Seb, what are you doing?" Ben asked, clearly confused, holding Duke's lead as he closed the kitchen door behind him.

"Starting with number one on my to-do list," Seb replied, glancing at his notebook. "Browse the internet for a bulb."

He looked back at Ben. "Mrs. Ashworth is adamant her Tiffany Trumpet lamp is looking rather dull and could blow at any given moment, so I have been tasked to find a backup. You can never be too prepared, I suppose." He sipped his coffee with an air of importance.

"No, sorry, I meant why are you doing it out here? Isn't that something you can do inside where it's warm and more comfortable?" Ben raised an eyebrow.

"I'm catching some vitamin D. It's extremely vital for the body!" Seb peered over his glasses, then gestured towards Danny with a wink and stuck his tongue out.

Danny, overhearing the conversation, shook his head and chuckled. "Seb, you do realise it's cloudy and about minus one, right?"

"I'm sure there's some sun up there somewhere. Besides, I need to stay vigilant in case any plants try to escape," he added, dramatically glancing around.

"Right, of course. Well, you carry on getting some of that non-existent sun. I'll catch you later," Ben said, trying to stifle a laugh as he walked down the garden steps and onto the grass.

Seb leaned back in his chair and whispered to himself, "Vitamin D and preparedness, the keys to success," before taking another satisfied sip of his coffee. "Oooh, before you go, would you like a lift to and from the pub later?" he shouted to Ben, who was already heading down the garden.

"A lift down would be great, but coming back is sorted, thanks, Seb. I've booked a taxi for ten o'clock."

"Why so early? Go and enjoy yourself! Whip that hair back and forth. It's your eighteenth, for goodness' sake!"

"It's not really my scene. I'm thankful I have friends that

want to celebrate with me, but I'm not too bothered, if I'm being completely honest."

"Well, it's your day. You have to do whatever you want to do. As long as you're happy, that's all that matters to us." Seb smiled at Ben.

"Right, well, I won't be long. Got some essays I need to finish if I want to get into my chosen university!" Ben mustered a smile in return, then slipped his headphones in his ears, and turned away before his composure faltered. With a deep breath, he set off. Duke was already ahead, sniffing the way.

"You think he's okay?" Danny looked at Seb.

"I think he's disheartened. Business is business. We know that, and Ben knows that, but it's his eighteenth. That only happens once."

"I wonder why Keith didn't take this trip on." Danny climbed down from the ladder.

"I was thinking the same. Wasn't hiring a managing director supposed to let Mr. Ashworth take a step back? He's not getting any younger."

Danny looked at Seb with a sardonic expression. "Mr. Ashworth taking a step back? That business is like another son to him. We all knew that would never happen."

"Hmm, you're not wrong." Seb tapped his fingers on the table.

Ben's morning run around the grounds was filled with a mix of emotions. As his feet rapidly pounded the familiar paths, his mind raced even faster. He couldn't shake the surprise and disappointment that his parents had chosen this particular time for a business trip. It wasn't unusual for his dad to embark on last-minute work travels, but today it stung more than usual. Even Ben, who was used to his father's unpredictable schedule, was taken aback that his parents decided to leave right before his eighteenth birthday.

The run passed in a blur. The usual landmarks—the old oak tree, the pond, the gardener's shed—seemed to be shrouded in a haze. His heart wasn't in it. He was hurt, and the physical exertion did little to clear his mind. Each step he took seemed to mirror the frustration and sadness building up inside him. He had hoped that turning eighteen would mark a special moment, a milestone celebrated with his family. Instead, he was left to process his feelings alone, with only the rhythmic sound of his breathing and the crunch of gravel underfoot to keep him company.

The early-morning light, usually a source of calm and clarity, did little to lift his spirits. The serene beauty of the grounds felt almost mocking as if highlighting the contrast between his internal turmoil and the peaceful surroundings. The solitude of the run gave him too much time to think, to mull over his parents' current absence. He couldn't help but feel a sense of abandonment and a nagging question echoed in his mind: Why wasn't he important enough for them to stay?

As he pushed through the final stretch of his run, his emotions remained a tangled mess. The physical fatigue started to set in, but it was the emotional exhaustion that weighed most heavily on him. Returning home, he knew he would have to face the day ahead, but the sting of his parents not being there would linger, a silent reminder of his unmet expectations and the complex reality of family dynamics.

Chapter Three

Seven o'clock rolled around, and the evening air was heavy with the chill of an early winter night. Seb carefully manoeuvred his car through the dimly lit village, the headlights cutting through the thick darkness as he pulled up to the front of the old stone-walled pub. The warm glow from inside spilled out into the cold, inviting those outside to seek refuge within its cosy embrace.

Ben was sitting in the passenger seat. He was bundled up in a conservative tweed coat that contrasted sharply with the unmistakably loud Prada shirt he wore underneath. The shirt, with its bold colours and intricate design, stood out vividly against the more muted tones of the evening. Since Seb was his ride for the night, Ben felt obliged to wear it, despite his initial reluctance.

"Thanks, Seb, I really appreciate the lift," Ben said, his breath visible in the cold air as he opened the car door.

Seb smiled, the corners of his eyes crinkling. "You're very welcome, dear. Have fun, and if you decide to stay longer, just text me. I've got no plans tonight. By the way, that shirt looks exquisite!" Seb gave him a cheeky wink, his eyes twinkling with mischief.

Ben chuckled, shaking his head. "I knew you'd say that. You always have a way of making me step out of my comfort zone."

"That's what friends are for, isn't it? To make sure you look fabulous, even when you don't feel like it." Seb grinned.

Ben nodded, a smile spreading across his face. "True, true. Well, I better get inside before we both freeze. Thanks again, Seb."

"No problem at all," Seb replied, watching as Ben got out of the car and made his way to the pub entrance.

The door opened, and the sound of laughter and clinking glasses floated out, mingling with the crisp night air. Ben gave a wave before disappearing inside.

Ben was greeted with a chorus of cheers from his friends, their faces lighting up with genuine delight at his arrival. The pub buzzed with energy. At the centre of the group stood Richard Coldwell, the unmistakable ringleader, whose boisterous laugh seemed to fill the entire room.

Richard was one of those larger-than-life characters who thrived on attention and always had to outdo everyone else. His stories were always a bit grander, his jokes a touch funnier, and his presence was impossible to ignore. Tonight was no exception. Draped in a velvet blazer and sporting a theatrical grin, Richard held court among their friends, regaling them with a tale that had everyone in stitches.

Richard's family, multi-billionaires thanks to Coldwell Shortbreads, founded in 1835, had managed to place their products in nearly every supermarket across Europe. Richard, sometimes called Dicky—and less affectionately, dickhead—had been Ben's best friend since prep school. However, while Richard still considered them best friends, Ben's feelings had changed over the years.

Ben's disillusionment with Richard had grown steadily, especially after seeing how he treated women, including his current girlfriend, Camilla, who was part of their circle of friends. Richard's charm and wealth often masked his flaws, but Ben couldn't ignore the casual disrespect and manipulation Richard exhibited. It was like watching a puppet show, where everyone danced to Richard's tune, blind to the strings he pulled.

Despite his growing discomfort, Ben stayed quiet about it. He avoided drama and confrontation, preferring to keep the peace rather than ignite conflict within the group. The pressure of unspoken words and unaddressed grievances hung heavy on his shoulders, but he convinced himself that it was better this way. Confronting Richard would mean shattering the fragile harmony of their friendship circle, and Ben wasn't ready to face the fallout.

Camilla's situation particularly gnawed at Ben. She was smart, kind, and deserved better than Richard's empty promises and thoughtless behaviour. Ben had seen the way Richard belittled her in private, and it made his blood boil. Yet, every time he considered saying something, he hesitated, unsure of how to broach the subject without causing a rift.

Ben's silence was both a shield and a prison. It protected him from the immediate chaos of confrontation but trapped him in a cycle of frustration and helplessness. He watched from the sidelines as Richard continued his charade, feeling increasingly disconnected from the person who had once been his closest confidant.

As Richard stepped forward to wrap his arms around Ben, he quickly wiped a white powdery residue from his nose. Ben recognised it immediately, and the sight only deepened his unease. He didn't agree with Richard's fondness for drug use, but there was nothing Ben could do or say to steer him away from them.

"Ben, you made it!" Richard boomed, his voice cutting through the chatter as he waved Ben over with exaggerated enthusiasm. "We were just talking about that time you nearly set the barbecue on fire!"

Ben rolled his eyes good-naturedly as he joined the group. "You mean the time *you* nearly set the barbecue on fire, Richard," he corrected, eliciting a round of laughter.

Richard threw his head back and guffawed heartily. "Details, details!" he exclaimed, smacking Ben on the back. "The important thing is, you're here now and the night is young!"

"Finally, the last of us to turn eighteen!" George exclaimed, raising his glass high, urging others to follow suit.

"Here's your favourite tipple. Cheers!" Richard handed Ben a pint of the local beer. The group toasted him, the clinking of glasses echoing through the pub.

"Thanks, everyone." Ben smiled and took a sip, savouring the familiar taste.

"Have you been up to much today, Ben?" Eric asked, leaning in.

"Not really. My parents left for a business trip early this morning, so I just went for my usual run and did some uni prep." Ben looked down at his pint, a mix of emotions swirling in his stomach.

"I have to say, interesting choice of shirt..." Richard laughed, nudging one of the other lads to join in.

Ben brushed himself down and shot back, "Hey, knock it off. Sebastian bought it for me to wear tonight. He dropped me off, so I had to wear it. I actually really like it. It's different."

"Speaking of different, who's the bird you've been texting tonight, Richard? Don't think we haven't noticed that keen smile." Aaron smirked.

Richard grinned, and puffed out his chest. "Just some catwalk model from London. Met her last weekend on my trip to Nottingham. She was fire."

"Oh, not Kendall Jenner this time?" Aaron joked, prompting more laughter from the group.

"No, she backed off after I turned her down twice." Richard fluffed his hair arrogantly, basking in the attention.

Ben glared at Richard, puzzled and increasingly irritated. "I'll never understand you."

"What do you mean?" Richard raised an eyebrow, feigning innocence.

"You have the most amazing girlfriend, yet you're always cheating on her. Why?" Ben asked, unable to contain himself any longer.

"Oh, shut up, Ben. The man's a god. Any girl, anytime. Don't tell me you wouldn't have it that way," Aaron jumped in before Richard could respond, his voice filled with misplaced admiration.

"Yeah, like, don't get me wrong, Camilla is top-notch, but I'm away a lot. I have needs." Richard winked and laughed, the rest of the lads joining in, their laughter grating on Ben's nerves.

"No, actually, funnily enough, I wouldn't have it that way at all," Ben replied firmly, his voice cutting through the din.

"God, Ben, stop. We're not old respectful men. We're eighteen-year-old chaps playing the field and having fun. Lighten up. Let's not fall out over this. It's your birthday. Come on, drink up!" Richard handed Ben another pint, trying to defuse the tension with forced cheerfulness.

Ben took the pint, his mind racing. The laughter and camaraderie of the group felt hollow, the evening tainted by the uncomfortable truths that had bubbled to the surface. He looked at Richard, his oldest friend, and realised that the man he once admired had become a stranger. The lines of loyalty and morality blurred in his mind, and he wondered how much longer he could stay silent.

Ben shook his head, picked up his pint, and wandered over to an empty table. He needed a moment away from the loud banter and conflicting emotions. As he settled into his seat, the pub door swung open and in walked Camilla with a group of friends. They looked stunning, their presence immediately drawing the attention of everyone in the room. They made their way to the bar where Richard and the lads were still standing, caught up in their own world.

"Good evening, gentlemen. How are we all?" Camilla asked, her voice cutting through the noise with a warm yet commanding tone.

"Much better now you lovely ladies are here," Richard declared, grabbing Camilla by the waist. He twirled her round dramatically before pulling her in for a kiss, an ostentatious display of affection. "Eric, order these ladies a drink."

Camilla scanned the room. "Where's the birthday boy?" she asked, looking for Ben.

"He's over there." Richard pointed with a dismissive wave. "A bit sensitive tonight. He's on his second beer." The lads laughed mockingly, their derision ringing in Ben's ears.

Camilla rolled her eyes at their immaturity and walked over to Ben. She sat opposite him, her presence a calming contrast to the raucous group at the bar. They chatted for a while, their conversation flowing easily. Camilla had a way of making Ben feel heard and understood; something he desperately needed tonight.

Unbeknownst to Camilla, she had cheered Ben up considerably. Her genuine interest and big smile were a balm to his troubled thoughts. However, after an hour, the noise and the emotional strain of the evening had taken their toll. Ben decided he was ready to go home.

He discreetly cancelled the taxi he had booked earlier and sent a quick text to Seb.

Ben stood up, thanked Camilla for her company and, with a forced smile, thanked the rest of the group. The boys barely acknowledged his departure, still engrossed in their own revelry.

Standing alone under the dim street lights, Ben's mind swirled with a mixture of relief and sadness. This birthday, meant to be a milestone, had been a harsh reminder of how much had changed. The friends he once held dear now felt like strangers, their laughter and camaraderie masking a deep disconnection. The realisation cut deep: the people he had grown up with, shared countless memories with, no longer understood or cared for the person he had become.

As Seb's car pulled up, Ben took a deep breath, trying to shake off the overwhelming sense of loneliness. The night air, though refreshing, couldn't wash away the sting of betrayal and the emptiness that had settled in his heart.

Climbing into the car, he gave Seb a grateful but weary smile, hoping he didn't notice the tears threatening to spill. The people who should have been there for him, who should have celebrated his life and his growth, were the ones who had made him feel the most alone.

Seb tried to strike up a conversation on the way home, but Ben was lost in his own thoughts, offering only absent-minded nods and half-hearted responses.

He was grateful that Seb left him to his thoughts and didn't push the conversation.

Chapter Four

It had been five days since Mr. and Mrs. Ashworth departed for their business trip, leaving the estate unusually quiet. Benedict, unable to resist the lure of curiosity, decided to explore his father's home office—a habit he indulged in whenever the house was empty. The room, a space once brimming with his father's presence, was now a solemn reminder of its occupant's absence.

Even though the family business was officially in his name, Ben was always adamant he didn't want to be involved until he had completed his degree in construction management. He was determined to prove himself worthy of the legacy he had now inherited. He aimed to secure a place at Cambridge this September, despite knowing the degree itself was not a necessity for his future role in the company. For Ben, it was crucial to demonstrate his value through personal achievement rather than merely relying on the inheritance of the family business.

As he walked around the room, his eyes scanned the meticulously organised shelves and the large oak desk, now silent without his father's daily activity. Each item seemed to hold a whisper of his father's influence: an array of neatly stacked papers, a leather-bound journal, and a well-worn armchair that had seen countless late-night meetings. Benedict's resolve grew stronger with each step he took through the room, as he felt the weight of both his father's legacy and his own ambitions.

The office was an expansive, richly appointed space. Believed to have once served as the estate's original billiard room, it was positioned prominently on the ground floor near the entrance. Its grand proportions and ornate details spoke to its storied past. Behind his father's mahogany desk, the back wall was adorned with the iconic Ward & Ashworth emblem, sitting proudly over the room. The office was outfitted with every professional amenity, including a sleek coffee machine flanked by personalised business mugs that hinted at the company's refined taste.

One wall was devoted to an elaborate display of photographs and framed newspaper clippings, meticulously arranged in chronological order. This gallery provided a vivid narrative of Warden Ashworth's journey from ambitious entrepreneur to founder of the thriving family business. Each piece of memorabilia captured a significant milestone, from early struggles to eventual triumphs.

Ben walked over to the wall of pictures, his gaze moving over each frame with quiet, almost reverent, intensity. Studying the images, he could almost hear his grandfather's voice, recounting each story as Ben would perch on his knee as a child.

At just twenty-two years old, Warden James Ashworth founded the family business in 1956. Driven by a profound passion for construction and a wealth of studied knowledge, despite no hands-on experience, he seized an incredible opportunity by acquiring a design and build contractor that had gone into liquidation. With vision and determination, he transformed a setback into the foundation of the family legacy.

Most days, Warden would be impeccably dressed in a sharp suit, sitting confidently at his polished desk, surrounded by equally distinguished gentlemen as he signed contract after contract. In 1959, following a bold investment in a visionary rebranding, he unveiled a magnificent new head office in the heart of London. The grand opening was a spectacle, drawing hundreds of onlookers and extensive media coverage. The pinnacle of the day came when a member of the royal family cut the ribbon, symbolising the dawn of a new era. This wasn't just the opening of a building but the realisation of a dream and the start of an inspiring journey.

Ward & Ashworth quickly became one of the UK's most prestigious design and build contractors, largely due to Warden's exceptional leadership. He built a team of nearly 150 skilled professionals, tackling projects ranging from residential complexes to major hotel groups. His knack for presenting compelling blueprints and securing contracts ensured a steady stream of successful projects. Though some might attribute his success to old money, his vision and dedication were clearly the driving force.

Warden eventually married his childhood sweetheart, Lillian, whose unwavering support was crucial to his accomplishments. In 1965, they welcomed their only child, Henry Magnus Ashworth. Balancing a thriving career with family life, Warden's days were spent traversing building sites, engaging in lengthy phone calls, and poring over contracts. It was the dynamic, fast-paced life he'd always wanted, but everything changed in 1977. Lillian's sudden death from Russian flu left him grief-stricken, and he decided to step back from the business to spend more time at home with young Henry. He converted a room of the house into an office—the same office that's still used today. Though Ben's grandfather had long since passed, Ben had never forgotten Warden's final wish: for the business to remain within the family, no matter what. That wish sparked Ben's own interest in construction.

Continuing his snoop, Ben walked over to his father's desk, its polished surface reflecting the soft glow of the study lamp. At first glance, nothing seemed unusual—a few sticky notes from meetings, neatly aligned fountain pens, and what appeared to be the current project his parents might have gone away for. Intrigued, he took a seat in the plush leather chair and began to flick through the papers. The project detailed a rural location in Scotland, an independent hotel entangled in a web of planning permission issues due to divided local opinions. The documents included architectural plans, correspondence from local officials, and handwritten notes. Among the sticky notes, one stood out: it had tomorrow's date and the words *residential consultation?* on it. This must be where his parents were.

Feeling a mix of curiosity and concern, Ben reached into his pocket and pulled out his mobile phone. He dialled his father's number, but it went straight to voicemail—likely due to the notoriously poor signal in rural Scotland. Undeterred, Ben continued to sift through the papers, hoping to find more clues about his parents' whereabouts.

Amid the documents, he found a printed email from the hotel's correspondence team. It contained a detailed itinerary and a Scottish area-coded number. Sensing this was his best lead, Ben picked up the phone and dialled, his fingers tapping impatiently on the desk as he waited for someone to answer.

The phone rang a few times before a voice on the other end picked up. "Good afternoon, Lode Inn site office. How may I help you?"

"Hello, my name is Benedict Ashworth from W&A. I wanted to confirm that Mr. and Mrs. Ashworth arrived safely for tomorrow's local consultation."

"Let me transfer you to the communications team. Hold, please."

Ben waited patiently, listening to the soft music. After a few moments, a new voice came on the line.

"Hello, Benedict. This is Hugh, head of communications. Thanks for calling. We're quite concerned as we expected the meeting to happen, but no one arrived on Monday as planned. It's now Friday, and negotiations with residents are supposed to be tomorrow. Mr. Ashworth has stopped responding to emails and calls. Given your business's reputation, this is disappointing. We want to proceed with blueprint B, but we need local approval."

Despite not being directly involved in the family business, Ben felt a wave of embarrassment wash over him. He responded quickly, trying to salvage the situation.

"Hello, Hugh. I sincerely apologise. There seems to be a huge mix-up on our end, and it's completely unacceptable. I know it's short notice, but could you still advertise the consultation for tomorrow? I'll send someone up today to handle it."

"Absolutely! That would be fantastic. We're excited to

work with you, and we appreciate your efforts to resolve this."

"It's the least we can do. We're looking forward to working with you too, despite the rough start. I'll be in touch." Ben hung up and took a deep breath.

He picked up a business card bearing his father's work number and dialled it, his fingers trembling slightly. The call was redirected after a few rings and Keith, the managing director, answered.

"Hey, Ben, what's up?" Keith asked, his tone a mixture of curiosity and concern.

"Hi, Keith, I'm having trouble reaching Ma and Pa. They're supposed to be in Scotland at the Lode Inn, but they aren't there. The communications manager is getting increasingly upset. I promised someone would be on-site today. You need to send someone ASAP!" Ben spoke with urgency.

"Oh bollocks," Keith cursed under his breath. "I've been so swamped with work that I've been ignoring calls from numbers I didn't recognise. I assumed they were there as planned. They must be somewhere else. With all the projects we have going on, it's been a nightmare keeping up."

"Don't worry, but we need someone there immediately. We can't afford to lose this contract," Ben insisted, his anxiety palpable.

"I'll send Stuart over right away. Can you gather all the relevant paperwork for me? He'll swing by and collect it," Keith replied, already sounding like he was shifting into action mode.

"Got it. I'll get everything together now. See you soon." Ben ended the call, his mind racing with the potential fallout from the mix-up. He quickly turned to the desk, sifting through the clutter with focused determination. Papers flew across the surface as he pulled together every document related to the Lode Inn project.

Each piece of paper felt like a puzzle piece in a larger, urgent task. Ben's thoughts swirled with concerns over the implications of the missed appointment. As he organised the documents into a neat stack, he couldn't shake the feeling of impending pressure. His renewed sense of urgency was matched by a relentless drive to ensure that nothing else would go wrong. With the paperwork assembled and his mind still reeling from the frantic phone call, he prepared for the imminent arrival of Stuart, determined to make sure everything would be handled with the utmost care.

Chapter Five

Slamming the door behind him with a resounding thud, Richard hastily pursued Camilla out to the front of his parents' stately home. The morning air was thick with fog and the early sunlight tried to cut through. Draped in a silk dressing gown and elegant slippers, Camilla stormed ahead, her face a mask of controlled fury. She struggled to manoeuvre her designer mini suitcase, its polished wheels gliding smoothly but hastily over the pristine gravel path. Her meticulously packed belongings were neatly arranged inside, the suitcase an extension of her refined yet hurried departure.

"Camilla, come back, please! Let me explain!" Richard shouted.

"You don't need to explain a thing. The text says everything."

"It doesn't! It's not like that. It's just banter. Trust me."

"Are you joking? You think sending an explicit photo to another girl while you're lying next to your girlfriend is banter? And I know it was yours because it bends to the right!"

"My dick does not bend to the right," Richard shouted, drawing the attention of two nearby gardeners, who looked at him with second-hand embarrassment. He adjusted his volume, his face partially red. "Anyway, I thought you were asleep."

"Oh, so me being asleep makes it okay?"

"No. I didn't mean to send that picture. I was supposed to send a picture of my new golf clubs to Eric, but somehow, the phone sent a picture of my dick to her. I don't even know how. Stupid fucking phone!"

"Oh my God, I wasn't born yesterday, you prick." Camilla wiped away a tear and moved to walk away. Richard reached out to grab her arm. "Don't even try to touch me. Leave me the fuck alone!" Camilla got in her car, and Richard watched her depart down the driveway. He was stunned but knew exactly what he had done. He walked back into the house.

"Thank goodness for that. I did not like her one bit!" Mrs. Coldwell sighed in relief, her voice shuddering with disdain as she turned away from the window. The tension in her shoulders eased visibly, and she smoothed an errant strand of hair back into place with a satisfied smile.

"Oh, she'll come back to me. They always do." Richard smirked, a self-satisfied gleam in his eyes. He leaned casually against the marble mantelpiece, exuding a confidence that bordered on arrogance, as if the world and everyone in it were merely players in his personal game.

"I hope not. No one will ever be good enough for my son," Mrs. Coldwell replied, her voice softening as she stepped closer to Richard. She cupped his face with both hands, her fingers tenderly tracing the contours of his cheeks before playfully bopping his nose. Her eyes sparkled with adoration, as if she were gazing upon a perfect work of art. In her eyes, Richard could do no wrong. He was the centre of her world, the golden boy who deserved nothing less than unconditional love and adoration. To Mrs. Coldwell, her son was flawless, a paragon of virtue that the rest of the world seemed foolishly blind to.

Across the room, Mr. Coldwell lowered his newspaper, his expression clouded with a mixture of disappointment and frustration. He sighed quietly, rolling his eyes discreetly at the exchange between his wife and son. Unlike his wife, he had seen potential in Camilla, believing she had the strength and character to mould Richard into something more than the spoiled, aimless man he had become—something Mr. Coldwell desperately yearned for. In Camilla, he had seen a chance for Richard to grow, to face the challenges of the real world, and to become a man worthy of the Coldwell name.

As his wife fussed over Richard, adjusting his collar and straightening his hair with a devotion that bordered on obsession, Mr. Coldwell couldn't help but feel a deep sense of regret. He folded his newspaper with a snap, the sound cutting through the room like a whip, and stood up, casting one last lingering look at his wife and son. To him, the sight was a painful reminder of all that had gone wrong. Mrs. Coldwell's love for Richard had crossed the line into worship, blinding her to his flaws and enabling his worst tendencies. Mr. Coldwell's affection for his son, on the other hand, had long been tempered by a stern, unyielding desire for Richard to grow up and take responsibility for his life. Camilla, in his eyes, had represented a bridge to that world— a world where Richard would have been forced to confront his shortcomings and become the man he was meant to be. But now, with that bridge burned, Mr. Coldwell could see only the widening chasm between himself and his son.

As he retreated to his study, leaving the mother and son in their cocoon of mutual admiration, Mr. Coldwell couldn't help but feel a growing sense of resentment. It was a resentment born from years of frustration and disappointment, from watching his son squander every opportunity and fall deeper into a life of excess. Richard had never truly been his son—not in the way a father hopes for. He was his mother's creation, a reflection of her blind adoration and indulgence.

The truth was, Richard and his father had never shared a good relationship. From the earliest days, there had been a wedge between them—a wedge that had grown larger over the years as Richard became more and more entangled in his mother's protective embrace. Mrs. Coldwell's unwavering devotion to her son had been a constant source of tension in the household, leading to countless arguments as she consistently put Richard first, even at the expense of her marriage. But Mr. Coldwell could see what she refused to acknowledge—the cracks in their relationship that were widening with each passing day.

What she didn't know was that Richard had been spiralling into drug use and using the family's money to fund his growing habit.

Mr. Coldwell had discovered the truth, and in a rare moment of desperation, Richard had begged his father not to tell his mother, promising to quit in exchange for his father's silence. But the promises had been empty, and the continued use of the family's finances, coupled with the risk to their reputation, had pushed Mr. Coldwell to the edge.

He had warned Richard, again and again, that if he didn't stop tarnishing the family name, he would find himself out on the streets, cut off from the family's fortune and forced to fend for himself. But the warning had fallen on deaf ears, as it always did. Richard had grown up with everything handed to him on a silver plate, and the idea of actually working for anything in life was as foreign to him as the notion of failure.

As Mr. Coldwell closed the door to his study, he couldn't shake the bitter thought that had been gnawing at him for years: he had failed as a father. He had failed to instil in his son the values that had made the Coldwell name one of honour and respect. And now, he feared, it was too late to fix what was broken. Richard was lost to him, a product of his mother's blind love and his own inability to bridge the gap between them. In that moment, as he sat alone in his study, Mr. Coldwell realised with a heavy heart that his resentment had grown into something darker—an anger that simmered just beneath the surface, fuelled by the knowledge that his son would never be the man he had hoped for.

It was a hatred born not of malice, but of disappointment—a deep, abiding disappointment in the boy who had once been his pride and joy, but who had become a man he could hardly bear to look at. Mr. Coldwell knew this was a wound that would never heal, a rift that would never be mended. The son he had once loved was gone, replaced by a stranger he no longer recognised, and the father he had once been had become a man filled with regret and bitterness, unable to forgive the one person he had hoped to save.

Benedict was out driving his sleek khaki green Range Rover when he received a call through the hands-free system. The familiar ringtone filled the car's interior, and the dashboard display showed it was Sally calling. He pressed a button on the steering wheel to answer.

"Hey, Sally, everything okay?" he asked.

"Hey, Ben, I don't suppose you could swing by the shop and grab some plain flour? I'm going to make your favourite garlic bread tonight, but I stupidly forgot to pick up another tub during the last shop." Sally's voice came through with an apologetic tone.

"Yes, of course, Chef! I'm coming up to it now, funnily enough," Benedict replied with a chuckle, glancing at the approaching shop ahead.

"Yes, I know, I tracked you!" Sally teased, her voice light and playful.

"Now that I'm eighteen, do you think we could turn the trackers off?" Ben laughed, trying to keep the conversation light-hearted, but there was a note of earnestness in his voice.

"As soon as your parents request it, I will. But you know what they'll say: 'You live under our roof, we need to know where you are', even if it is through me!" Sally responded, mimicking his parents' stern tone before breaking into a laugh.

"But technically, I'm the owner of the house now, so surely I have that decision?" Ben argued, smiling at his clever loophole.

"Hmm, smart. I guess you're right. Switching off now! Just don't forget the flour, please!" Sally conceded, her tone a mix of amusement and admiration for his quick thinking.

"I won't! Going in now. See you soon," Ben replied as he pulled into the shop's car park. The call ended with a beep, and Ben parked, then stepped out of the car into the afternoon sun.

He walked briskly towards the store, the automatic doors sliding open to welcome him into the warm interior. The familiar layout was a comfort, and he made his way to the baking aisle. As he reached for a tub of plain flour, he couldn't help but smile at the thought of Sally preparing his favourite garlic bread. It was a simple gesture, but it made him feel cared for.

With the flour in his basket, Ben took a moment to look around, recognising a few familiar faces and exchanging polite nods. He headed to the checkout, the cashier greeting him with a friendly smile as she scanned the flour.

As Ben headed out of the shop, he accidentally bumped into Camilla on her way in. She looked a total mess, tears streaming down her face and still in nightwear, her usually impeccable appearance now dishevelled.

"Camilla, what on earth's wrong?" Ben exclaimed, instinctively pulling her close to his chest in a comforting embrace.

"I'm just having a really bad day," she mumbled, her voice breaking as she tried to hold back more tears.

"Look, here are my keys. Go wait in my car," Ben said. She took them, wiped her face with her hand, and managed a heartfelt, albeit weak, smile.

Ben watched her walk towards his car before he turned back into the store. He hurried through the aisles, grabbing a bar of chocolate. He paid quickly, his mind racing with concern for Camilla. Clutching the flour and chocolate bar, he made his way back to his Range Rover where Camilla was sitting in the passenger seat, looking lost and forlorn.

"Speak to me. What's happened?" he asked gently, handing her the chocolate.

"Thank you, Ben," she said, managing a slight smile. "I've split from Richard, but I'm not sad about that. He's a knobhead. It's just the principle and how he's made me feel."

"I've known Richard my whole life. Growing up, I saw every behaviour possible with him and women. He is a right knobhead. I almost want to ask what could he possibly have done now because I don't think there's anything he hasn't done, if I'm being honest," Ben replied, shaking his head.

"I was lying next to him and had just woken up. He was on his phone, sending a dick pic to some blonde girl on WhatsApp. Then he had the audacity to say it was his phone glitching and that it was supposed to be a picture of his new golf clubs to Eric..." Camilla's voice wavered between anger and disbelief.

"Well, that certainly is a new one! To think he thought that would even work is beyond me!" Ben said, rolling his eyes.

"To think I thought we'd work as a couple. We're so, so different. I'm so against drugs too. I was obviously blinded by all the fancy restaurants and luxury holidays we went on and got caught up in it all. He's actually an awful person the more I think about it," Camilla mused, her voice steadier now.

"I agree with you there. He is an awful person. I know we're best friends but it's not been like that for a very long time now. He's really arrogant and thinks because he's good-looking and from one of the richest families in England, he can get any girl but then doesn't appreciate a good girl when he has one. Like you, for example," Ben said earnestly.

Camilla smiled, a genuine smile this time. "Thank you, Ben. I appreciate it. The chat and chocolate really helped. But I'm lactose intolerant, so I best leave this here." She leaned in to kiss Ben on the cheek and got out of the car.

"Ah, why do I feel like I should know that..." Ben muttered, feeling slightly embarrassed.

"We've only been in the same friendship group since the middle of boarding school," she teased, winking as she shut the car door.

Ben smiled, shook his head, and tore open the chocolate before starting up his car to head home. The rich aroma of the chocolate filled the car as he took a bite, the sweetness mingling with the lingering warmth of Camilla's kiss on his cheek. He savoured the moment, but his thoughts soon drifted back to her. The image of her tear-streaked face and the pain in her eyes tugged at his heartstrings, and he couldn't help but feel a surge of protection towards her.

As he drove, the familiar countryside scenery passed by, but his mind was elsewhere. He replayed their conversation, each word echoing in his head. Camilla deserved so much better than Richard. She was kind, intelligent, all genuine qualities that Richard, with his arrogance and superficial charm, could never truly appreciate.

Ben remembered the first time he met Camilla, back in boarding school. She had been a breath of fresh air in a world full of pretentiousness and social climbing. Her laugh was infectious, her smile bright enough to light up even the dreariest of days. Over the years, they had shared countless memories, from late-night study sessions to spontaneous road trips. She had always been there for him, a constant in his life, and seeing her hurt now stirred something deep within him.

As he navigated through the winding roads, Ben thought about how Richard had always taken Camilla for granted. The fancy restaurants, luxury holidays, and expensive gifts had been distractions, superficial gestures masking a lack of genuine affection and respect. Ben felt a wave of anger towards Richard, but it was quickly replaced by a resolve to be there for Camilla, to support her through this tough time.

The car's engine hummed softly, the rhythmic sound providing a backdrop to his thoughts. He imagined what it would be like if he were the one to make Camilla smile, to be the one she turned to, not out of necessity, but out of choice. The thought pleased him, but he quickly pushed it aside, focusing instead on the immediate task of being a good friend.

As Ben pulled into the driveway of his home, he took a deep breath and turned off the engine. The house loomed in front of him, a place that had recently become his responsibility. He glanced at the empty passenger seat beside him and sighed, wishing Camilla had stayed longer so he could offer more comfort.

Gathering the flour and the last of the chocolate, Ben made his way inside. The aroma of Sally's cooking was already drifting through the halls.

Chapter Six

Evening soon came. It was dark and chilly outside, but gathered in the dining room, fire lit, were the staff and Benedict. They were seated around an antique table that was gifted to his great-grandparents by King Christian X of Denmark in 1920. This furniture was not only valuable in price but also rich with sentimental history, a cherished family heirloom.

In front of each person was a plate of Chef Sally's homemade spaghetti bolognese. The rich aroma of tomatoes, ground beef, and herbs wafted through the air. Beside each plate was a slice of golden buttery garlic bread, its edges perfectly crisp. Each place setting included a glass of water and a glass of rich red wine. The deep hue of the wine caught the flickering firelight, adding a touch of elegance to the rustic meal.

Such communal dinners were a familiar and cherished part of life in the Ashworth household. The family and staff often dined together, sharing stories and laughter in a relaxed atmosphere. This practice was only set aside when the

Ashworths had guests or when the staff had plans outside the estate. This tradition of shared meals fostered a deep sense of unity and equality, blurring the lines between employer and employee. Everyone at the table was treated with the same respect, creating a strong, supportive community within the estate.

For once they ate in silence, nothing but the sound of the clinking of cutlery and the crackling of the fire filled the room. "This is gorgeous, Sally," Ben said, trying to maintain a casual tone.

"Aw, thank you, Ben. I'm glad you're enjoying it." Sally smiled at him.

The clinking continued in an uneasy rhythm.

"I think I want to call the police," Ben abruptly announced, his voice cutting through the quiet.

Sally's smile faded. "Oh, and where's that come from?" she asked, her worry evident.

Ben set down his fork. "I was in Pa's office this morning and tried calling the place I thought they'd been the last five days, but according to the company, they never arrived. I've called his mobile, but it doesn't ring. His work phone is set to divert to Keith, who now assumes they've gone elsewhere. I know Pa can be unpredictable, but something doesn't sit right with this."

"If you want to call them, we'll support that," Sally said, squeezing his arm in reassurance. "I agree, it does sound a bit odd, but also not, at the same time. Your father really is one of a kind. He's probably gone to a job and then headed off on a cruise somewhere in the Mediterranean."

Ben nodded slowly, but the worry in his eyes remained.

"Oh, I do hope not! I told him I *must* attend the next cruise. You know, be there in case they need anything." Seb

The Crimes of Middlemoor Estate

widened his eyes dramatically, though everyone knew he just wanted a vacation.

"It won't hurt to inform the police if you're not happy, Ben," Karin said, her voice firm as she looked over at him. "Ultimately, you've tried to contact them, you can't get through, and it's been longer than usual. I think it's a good idea."

"Yeah, I do too," Danny, a man of few words, added gravely.

"I can do it if you want, Ben?" Terry offered, his tone serious.

"No, it's okay. I'll... I'll do it," Ben replied, his voice shaky. He stood up, the seriousness of the situation pressing down on him, and left the room with a sense of urgency. The others watched him go, the worry in the air thickening.

As he entered the kitchen, a surge of anxiety made Ben's stomach churn. He headed for the housekeeper's phone, the first and only rotary phone installed in the house. Its vintage dial clicked as he called the non-emergency number, his heart pounding with each revolution.

The recorded message informed him there was an estimated wait time of eight minutes. Each second felt like an eternity as the silence of the kitchen amplified his unease. Anticipation gnawed at him, turning those eight minutes into what felt like an unending stretch of dread.

Sally poked her head around the kitchen door, her face showing concern. She gave a tentative thumbs-up, silently asking if everything was okay. Ben, forcing a shaky smile, mirrored her gesture, but the tension in his eyes betrayed him. Finally, after what seemed like an age, a voice on the other end answered. Ben's breath caught as he prepared to explain the unsettling situation, the gravity of his decision sinking in.

"Hello, you've reached the 101 non-emergency number for Devon. May I please start by taking your full name and current location?" the operator inquired.

"Hi, my name is Benedict George Ashworth, and I'm calling from Middlemoor Estate, Holland Grove Lane, Middlemoor, PL7 5PR," Benedict responded.

"Thank you, Benedict. How can I assist you today?" the operator asked, maintaining a calm and professional tone.

"I'm ringing to express concerns I have about my parents. I'm unsure if this is the right channel, but something doesn't seem right, and I'm quite worried," Benedict explained, trying to keep his voice steady.

"Understood. That's what we're here for. Could you please provide more details about your concerns?" the operator asked.

"Well," Benedict began, "they left for a business trip five days ago, and since then, I've been unable to reach them. I've tried calling their phones, but there's no answer. I contacted the company they were supposed to visit, but according to them, my parents never arrived. My father's business partner, Keith, mentioned they might be somewhere else, but we've no idea where that could be. The situation feels very unusual and troubling."

"You've made the right decision to call us. We'll initiate an investigation into their whereabouts. I can arrange for officers to come to your home within the hour to gather more information and assist you further. Will you be available to meet with them?"

"Yes, absolutely. I'll be here and ready to provide any

additional information they might need," Benedict confirmed.

"Great. Could you also arrange for Keith to come over as well? His input might be helpful in understanding the situation better."

"Certainly. I'll make sure he's informed and here as soon as possible," Benedict agreed, relieved to have some steps in motion. "Thank you for your assistance."

Ben hung up and took a deep breath, trying to calm his nerves. He turned to Sally, who had been waiting patiently in the doorway, her expression a mixture of concern and curiosity. He cracked a slight smile of relief, trying to reassure her. "They're sending officers over," he said, his voice carrying a hint of gratitude.

※

Within forty-five minutes, Terry, who had been keeping an eye on his security app, received a notification indicating someone was at the front gate. Glancing at the screen, he saw the familiar image of a police car, closely followed by Keith's vehicle. Terry's heart skipped a beat; the arrival of the police was an important step towards discovering what had happened to the Ashworths.

With a sense of purpose, Terry made his way to the front door. He opened it, allowing the police officers and Keith to enter. The officers offered polite nods and greetings as Keith followed closely behind them.

"Thank you for coming so promptly," Terry said. "Please

come in. I'll take you to the dining room where everyone is gathered."

As they moved through the house, Terry led them down the hallway. He made sure to keep the atmosphere as calm and organised as possible. Reaching the dining room, Terry opened the door and ushered the officers and Keith inside.

"Everyone, this is Detective Sergeant Ransome and Officer Lockwood," Terry introduced them, motioning towards the two officers who had come to assist.

The DS began. "Good evening, everyone. The high-profile nature of your family and the likely press interest in this case mean that I, as a Detective Sergeant, am here to ensure this inquiry is handled with the utmost care and priority. To start, I need to record everyone's names and their connections to Mr. and Mrs. Ashworth."

Once all the connections were established, Ransome proceeded with individual interviews in the kitchen. Hours passed, and as the early hours of the next morning approached, only Keith and Terry remained to be interviewed.

"Keith," the DS began, "could you please tell me what you know about the situation and whether you've been in contact with either Mr. or Mrs. Ashworth?"

Keith took a deep breath before responding. "I wasn't aware that Mr. Ashworth had set his calls to divert to me. He usually informs me about such changes, but this time he didn't. I've been receiving a number of calls from Scottish area codes, which I ignored because they seemed unfamiliar. I only answer calls from people I've saved in my contacts. It turns out that one of those calls was from the location where I initially thought Mr. and Mrs. Ashworth were. However, it appears they weren't there after all. I ended up having to send another employee to cover the job at the last minute."

The atmosphere in the room remained tense, but the process of gathering details was crucial for piecing together the missing pieces in the investigation.

"Do you have any idea where they might be instead?" the DS asked, trying to probe further.

Keith shook his head. "Honestly, no. This is one of the most challenging aspects of working with Mr. Ashworth. He's very independent and doesn't follow a set pattern. He often changes his plans without informing anyone. There was one time he left for a meeting so abruptly that by the time I managed to reach him, he had already flown to Las Vegas, checked into a hotel with Mrs. Ashworth, and settled in. This kind of unpredictability is actually quite normal for him, so I'm not sure why Ben felt the need to involve the police."

"Understood. What about his work habits? Does he frequently neglect his responsibilities or lose clients due to his erratic behaviour?"

"Not at all," Keith responded. "In fact, that's one aspect I find somewhat peculiar. Despite his unpredictable nature, he's always managed to keep everything running smoothly. There are times when he sends someone else in his place for meetings or events. He doesn't need to work in the conventional sense; our company is highly successful and well-established. For him, it's almost like a hobby or a passion project—another venture to oversee and engage with."

The DS nodded thoughtfully. "Okay. Could you please have Terry come in next?"

Keith left the kitchen to find Terry.

After a brief moment, Terry entered the room and took the chair that Keith had just vacated. Feeling slightly intimidated by the ongoing investigation, Terry took a deep breath, bracing himself for the questions ahead.

"Terry, could you please start by telling me the last time you saw Mr. and Mrs. Ashworth?" Detective Sergeant Ransome asked, turning a page in his notebook.

Terry adjusted his position in the chair and thought back. "The last time I saw them was the night before they left for their trip. Mr. Ashworth specifically asked me to leave the front gates open because they were departing in the early hours and didn't want to disturb me. As their request was important, and given his position as the boss, I agreed, though I'm not particularly comfortable doing so. It's against my usual protocol."

"I see. Is there any CCTV footage from the front gates that could help us establish the exact timing of their departure?" DS Ransome inquired, hoping to pinpoint the timeline more accurately.

"Yes, there's CCTV coverage," Terry replied. "I can access it from my phone. Just give me a moment."

Terry retrieved his phone from his pocket and launched the security app. He quickly entered the estate's password and navigated to the section for past recordings. As he selected the date for the night in question, his brow furrowed. "Hmm, that's strange. Normally, when you enter a specific date, the app displays the entire twenty-four-hour period of that day."

DS Ransome looked at the screen, his interest piqued. "Is there a possibility the system could have been switched off?"

"No, absolutely not," Terry responded with conviction. "I'm the only one with access to the security software, and I can assure you that the cameras are always on. They're crucial for the safety of the family and the estate."

"Could the app have experienced a glitch?" Officer Lockwood suggested.

"I doubt it," Terry said, shaking his head. "I've never had any issues with it before. I don't know what might have gone wrong this time. The best course of action would be to contact the help centre first thing tomorrow morning to try to resolve this."

DS Ransome's expression turned serious. "We need that recording as evidence to establish the exact times and details of their departure. Do you know if they used a taxi service?"

"Based on what I know, they must have used a taxi. All of their cars are here, so they definitely didn't drive themselves."

"Do you happen to know which taxi firm they normally use?" DS Ransome asked.

"Yes, they typically use Russell's in Tavistock. It's a local firm."

"Alright. I think we have everything we need for now," DS Ransome concluded. "I need you to contact the security help centre tomorrow and retrieve that recording as soon as possible. For now, we're done here."

Detective Sergeant Ransome and Officer Lockwood gathered their notes and prepared to leave. Terry and the officers made their way back to the dining room, where the remaining family members were visibly fatigued. The officers bid their farewells, promising to be in touch the following day with further instructions.

As the police departed, the family dispersed. Exhausted, Ben finally crawled into bed at 3.30 a.m. Despite his fatigue, he took a moment to send a text to Camilla, asking if she would be interested in a late-morning walk with the dogs. He felt a pressing need to get some fresh air and clear his mind.

Ben set his alarm for 9 a.m. He reached over to switch off his night light, casting the room into darkness. As he rolled over, his mind was a whirlwind of thoughts and concerns. The events of the past few hours replayed in his mind—each detail of the investigation, the police interviews, and the unnerving uncertainty of his parents' whereabouts.

He tried to push these thoughts aside, focusing instead on the rhythmic rise and fall of his breathing, hoping that rest would come despite the force of his worries. The silence of the house seemed almost oppressive, each creak of the floorboards or distant drone of the heating system echoed throughout. The image of the police officers taking notes, the perplexing issues with the CCTV footage, and Keith's detailed but unhelpful responses all swirled together in his mind.

In an attempt to calm his racing thoughts, Ben focused on the mundane tasks of the coming day. The thought of a walk with Camilla and the dogs was a small beacon of normality amidst the storm. Fresh air and a conversation with a good friend might help clear his head and provide some much-needed perspective.

Gradually, the exhaustion began to take over, and Ben's

thoughts became less coherent. He surrendered to the weariness, letting the day's stress melt into the comfort of sleep. He knew that tomorrow would bring new challenges, but with every passing hour, the investigation would inch closer to uncovering the truth. With this comforting thought, he allowed himself to drift off, hoping for a breakthrough in the morning and a chance to finally piece together the puzzle of his parents' disappearance.

Chapter Seven

What felt like a mere two minutes of sleep turned into morning far too quickly. A loud beep from his phone roused Ben from his fitful slumber. He blinked groggily, struggling to shake off the remnants of his restless night, but the promise of a new day and the need to face it head-on quickly took over. He picked up his phone and saw a message from Camilla. She was already up and ready for their morning walk.

He made his way to the kitchen, his footsteps echoing softly through the silent corridors of the grand estate. The morning sun was beginning to filter through the large windows, radiating a glow over the old polished wooden floors and antique furniture.

With a sigh, Ben prepared a quick breakfast. He sat at the table, stirring his cereal absent-mindedly, his thoughts drifting back to last night. As he ate, the house began to stir with activity. The distant sounds of doors opening and closing, muffled conversations, and the soft buzz of morning routines slowly filled the air. Sally entered the kitchen.

The Crimes of Middlemoor Estate

"Good morning, Ben," she greeted, as she moved around the kitchen. "I hope you slept well."

"Morning, Sally," Ben replied, managing a small smile. "As well as can be expected."

Sally glanced at his meagre breakfast and shook her head. "That won't do at all. Let me make you a proper breakfast. You need your strength."

Before Ben could protest, Sally had already set to work, cracking eggs into a bowl and whisking them vigorously. Her hands deftly prepared the ingredients for a more substantial meal. Within minutes, the kitchen was filled with the mouthwatering aroma of sizzling bacon and freshly baked bread.

As the morning progressed, the rest of the household began to appear. Karin walked in, her face showing signs of concern that she tried to mask with a veneer of calm. She gave Ben a reassuring smile and started to help Sally with the breakfast preparations. Danny, carrying a toolbox, entered shortly after, nodding to Ben as he poured himself a coffee. Seb arrived last, his usual energy slightly dampened by the prevailing sense of unease.

Despite the activity, there was an air of concern hanging over the house. The unexplained absence of Ben's parents caused a heavy cloud that affected everyone.

As they all settled around the kitchen table, Sally served up a hearty breakfast—scrambled eggs, crispy bacon, fresh tomatoes, and thick slices of toast.

"Thanks, Sally," Ben said appreciatively. "This is just what I needed."

"You're welcome, dear. We all need to keep our strength up. There's a lot to deal with."

Conversation at the table was a mix of mundane topics

and cautious optimism. They discussed the day's plans and the tasks that needed attention around the estate.

With breakfast finished, Ben turned his attention to Duke. He quickly harnessed the dog and loaded him into the car, eager to escape the confines of the house and clear his head. The car ride was a welcome distraction, the rhythmic noise of the engine a soothing backdrop to his thoughts.

Ben's destination was Lydford Gorge, a picturesque National Trust site renowned for its natural beauty and tranquil setting. Camilla had also been navigating her own challenges recently, and Ben felt that walking might help both of them find some solace.

As he drove, the landscape began to change as the village houses gave way to rolling countryside and the dense lush greenery of the gorge. The anticipation of reaching their meeting spot gave Ben a small but significant sense of relief. He pulled into the parking area, where he saw Camilla's car.

Camilla was waiting by the entrance to the gorge with her dog, Sibel. Her face lit up with a smile when she saw Ben. They greeted each other with a hug, a gesture that conveyed mutual understanding and support. Ben could see the weariness in Camilla's face. It mirrored his own exhaustion.

As they strolled along the winding path through Lydford Gorge with Duke and Sibel trotting cheerfully beside them, Camilla glanced at Ben, concern in her eyes. She broke the peaceful silence.

"How are you doing, Ben? You seem a bit... off."

Ben let out a sigh and ran a hand through his hair. "I reported my parents missing last night."

Camilla stopped in her tracks and stared at him. "Wait—what? Missing? Are you serious?"

He nodded, looking down at the trail. "Yeah. The whole thing is strange. I've been handed everything from the estate to the business and I can't get hold of them. I've no idea where they are. I felt like things weren't adding up, so I called it in, just to be cautious."

Camilla put a hand on his arm, her brow furrowed with worry. "Ben, that's huge. Do you really think something's wrong?"

He shrugged, trying to keep his tone light. "I hope not. Hopefully, I'm just overreacting, and they're fine. But I needed to take some kind of precaution, you know? Just to be safe."

Camilla nodded, still processing the news. "Well, I'm glad you did. And whatever happens, I'm here for you, okay?"

Ben gave her a small, grateful smile. "Thanks, Camilla. I think I just needed someone else to know... Hopefully, it's nothing, and they'll turn up soon."

Camilla returned his smile, her expression full of hope for Ben and his difficult situation. After a pause, she glanced at the rushing river. "You know, sometimes I wonder what things would have been like if my father had stuck around."

"I've never heard you talk about him before."

"Yeah, I guess I don't. He was... well, he was complicated. William was from this really wealthy family, and he met my mum, Caroline, at university. They were in love, or so she thought. But when she found out she was pregnant with me, he panicked and abandoned her."

"I'm sorry, Camilla. That must've been hard for her."

"It was. But my mum was so strong," Camilla replied, a note of pride in her voice. "She raised me all on her own, without any help from him—except for the trust fund he set up for my education. I think he wanted to appease his guilt without actually being a part of our lives."

Ben nodded thoughtfully. "And you never reached out to him?"

"No," Camilla said firmly. "I couldn't. He may have helped with my education, but he broke my mother's heart. That was enough for me to know he wasn't someone I wanted in my life." She looked down at Sibel, giving her a gentle scratch behind the ears. "Mum gave me everything. I didn't need him."

Ben smiled. "Sounds like your mum's resilience rubbed off on you, too."

Camilla laughed. "Maybe. She always made sure I felt loved and supported, even when things were tight. I think that's why I never felt his absence. It was just me and her, and that was more than enough."

Ben's gaze lingered on her, admiring her quiet strength. "You know, Camilla, that's one of the things I admire most about you. You've gone through so much, but you don't let it weigh you down."

"Thanks, Ben. I guess we're both navigating a lot right now. It's nice to be here together, to have someone who gets it."

They continued along the trail, the natural beauty around them easing some of the tension they'd both been carrying. Their footsteps were steady, the landscape serene, and for a short while, they felt that maybe, just maybe, they could find their way through their own challenges.

At the end of their walk, Ben and Camilla sat on a large rock near their parked cars and pulled off their muddy boots. Their hike had left their footwear caked in dirt, a testament to the rugged beauty of the trail they'd just conquered. Nearby, Duke and Sibel lay panting contentedly, tongues lolling as they recovered from the invigorating walk.

Camilla took in the lush surroundings and sighed. "I love it here. It's beautiful, and you can just switch off from everything. I hope the walk helped, Ben. I'm really sorry you're going through all of this."

"The walk definitely helped," Ben replied, his tone noticeably lighter than it had been in days. "It's good to get a break, even for a little while. But... back to reality, I guess. I should get home and see what's next."

"Of course. Just remember, I'm here if you need me. Text or call anytime."

"Thanks, Camilla." Ben gave her a hug. As they pulled apart and began to head to their cars, Ben hesitated, a thought crossing his mind.

"What are you doing tonight?" he asked, his tone carrying a note of hopeful curiosity.

"Nothing planned. Why?"

"I'll pick you up at seven," he suggested, his voice brightening. "Dinner at the Cornish Arms?"

Camilla's face lit up with a smile. "I'd really like that."

"Great," he said with a playful wink. "It's a date."

With a final wave, they parted ways and climbed into their cars. As Ben glanced back, watching Camilla and Sibel settle in, he felt a flicker of happiness amid the uncertainty. The thought of the evening ahead was a welcome distraction, a glimmer of something to look forward to. Starting his car, he felt a renewed sense of optimism. The road ahead might still be uncertain, but moments like these made it all feel a little more bearable.

TAVISTOCK HERITAGE & HILLS

Mysterious Disappearance of Mr. and Mrs. Ashworth Sends Shockwaves Through Quiet Devon Community

The sudden disappearance of Mr. and Mrs. Ashworth has left close ones and the local community shaken. The couple, well-known for their reclusive but prosperous lifestyle, vanished without a trace five days ago, leaving behind more questions than answers.

Benedict Ashworth, the couple's son, first raised the alarm after failing to reach his parents after their planned business trip. Their phones went unanswered, and the company they were supposed to visit confirmed they never arrived. Even more troubling was that Mr. Ashworth had set his work phone to divert calls to his business partner, Keith, who seemed equally baffled by their sudden absence.

Mr. Ashworth is said to be known as unpredictable and make last-minute scattered plans but even the staff of Middlemoor have expressed, this is not like him.

Local residents are now asking: Is something more sinister at play? The Ashworths, a wealthy and secretive couple, had long been known for their love of spontaneous trips, but this sudden disappearance is unlike anything their friends and employees have witnessed before.

As the investigation continues, the family remains on edge, waiting for answers to what could be a simple case of unpredictability or something far darker. Meanwhile, with the clock ticking and the mystery deepening, the once-peaceful estate now stands as the epicentre of a gripping tale that has left the village of Middlemoor on high alert.

With no clear leads and the unsettling absence of critical evidence, the question on everyone's lips is: Where are Mr. and Mrs. Ashworth? And will they ever return?

Chapter Eight

Terry sat at his desk, concerned as he dialled the security helpline. Each ring amplified his anxiety, his thoughts spiralling around the missing CCTV footage. The absence of these crucial recordings not only puzzled him but also made him feel vulnerable and a little bit culpable. The unanswered questions were a cacophony in his mind: How had the footage vanished? Who could be responsible? What would the implications be?

Finally, the call connected, and a wave of relief washed over him at the sound of a human voice.

"Good morning, you're through to SafeCapacity. My name is Becca. How may I assist you today?"

"Good morning," Terry began. "I'm urgently trying to review some CCTV footage from the beginning of this week, but nothing appears on my app or computer. It seems there might have been a glitch in the system."

"Okay, let's start with the basics. Could you please provide the address where the system is installed?"

"Middlemoor Estate, Holland Grove Lane, Middlemoor, PL7 5PR."

"Perfect. Can I have the name of the sole operator and the passcode associated with the system?"

"Yes, it's Terry Clover, and the passcode is 190721."

"Thank you. I'll just pull up your details... What specific day are you trying to review?"

"The early hours of Monday morning."

"Understood. One moment, please... It appears the system was placed on a six-hour time-out from 11.28 p.m. on Sunday to 05.28 a.m. on Monday."

"What does that mean?" Terry questioned as he tried to make sense of this new information.

"It's an eco feature that allows the system to turn off and stop recording to conserve energy. It was added last year following customer feedback."

"But I never activated that feature. Could this have been a system glitch?"

"No, our diagnostics would have flagged any anomalies. The records indicate that someone manually activated this feature. Is there a possibility that someone else knows your passcode?"

"I'm the sole operator," Terry replied, his mind racing to find an explanation. "No one else should have access to the system."

"Understood. Could it be possible that someone gained unauthorised access?"

Terry pondered this. "I suppose it's possible, but unlikely. I'm very cautious with the security protocols."

"I see. I can email you a chart showing the recorded hours and the activation of the eco feature."

"Yes, that would be helpful. Thank you."

The Crimes of Middlemoor Estate

As Terry ended the call, he leaned back in his chair, bewildered. He stared blankly at the ceiling. If no one else had access to the system, how had this happened? The more he thought about it, the more sinister the situation seemed.

An email notification from SafeCapacity ended his reverie. He opened it to find the chart Becca had mentioned. It clearly showed the system's downtime, aligning perfectly with the missing footage window. This wasn't a glitch; it was a deliberate action.

Terry's mind reeled with possibilities. Could someone have hacked into the system? Or perhaps there was an inside job at SafeCapacity itself? Every scenario seemed to point to some form of deliberate wrongdoing.

He couldn't help but wonder what the police would make of this. He had already been questioned about the missing footage, and this new information might shift their focus. But would it be enough to clear his own name, or would it complicate things further?

With a deep sigh, Terry closed his eyes, trying to piece together the puzzle. He needed to investigate further, but he had to be careful. Any misstep could lead to serious repercussions.

He stood up, pacing the room to clear his head. The office walls seemed to close in with each unanswered question. As the clock ticked, he resolved to take immediate action. First, he would secure all his personal accounts and change his passwords. Then, he would reach out to a cybersecurity expert to check for any signs of hacking. Finally, he would present his findings to the police, ensuring they had all the information needed to follow up on this mysterious and troubling situation.

With a plan forming in his mind, Terry felt a renewed

sense of purpose. This was just the beginning of unravelling the mystery, and he was determined to see it through.

Chapter Nine

Karin stepped into the library, a magnificent room that exuded an aura of timeless elegance and scholarly pursuit. The walls were adorned with dark wood panelling, rich with the patina of age, and the marks of countless hands that had brushed against them over the centuries. Towering shelves lined the room, stretching from the floor to the lofty ceiling, each shelf brimming with a vast collection of valuable books. These volumes, some with gilded spines and others bound in rich, cracked leather, hinted at the vast knowledge and history contained within their pages. Together, the books added up to millions in worth, making the library not just a sanctuary of knowledge, but a treasure trove of literary wealth.

The air was thick with the scent of old leather mingling with the subtle aroma of polished wood and the faint musty hint of ageing paper. It was a scent that spoke of countless hours spent in quiet contemplation and study.

The light that could enter through the windows was

minimal, prevented for the protection of the books. Yet, it danced across the intricately woven patterns of the antique Persian rug that covered the wooden floor. It also illuminated the elaborate carvings of the grand wooden fireplace that dominated the room's centre.

The fireplace itself was a masterpiece, its mantel adorned with detailed scenes from classical mythology, each figure painstakingly carved by artisans long gone. Above it hung a massive oil painting, its colours vibrant despite its age, depicting an ancestral figure with a stern countenance who seemed to watch over the room with a protective gaze. Plush armchairs and a sturdy mahogany writing desk completed the room, inviting anyone who entered to sit, read, and perhaps lose themselves in the labyrinth of knowledge that surrounded them.

As Karin moved methodically through her cleaning routine, she knelt down by the fireplace, her mind drifting as she dusted and polished. The crackling of the logs as she swept was soothing, almost rhythmic, providing a comforting background noise that made her tasks feel almost meditative. She carefully cleaned each nook and cranny, admiring the craftsmanship of the mantelpiece as she worked.

Suddenly, a faint but persistent scratching noise broke her concentration. The sound was coming from the direction of one of the bookcases. She paused, listening intently, trying to pinpoint the exact source of the noise. The scratching continued, faint but unmistakable, and a shiver ran down her spine.

Must be rats, she thought with a sigh, imagining the little pests scurrying behind the walls and nibbling at the wooden beams. The idea of rodents in such a grand and historic room was disheartening, but not entirely surprising given the

The Crimes of Middlemoor Estate

estate's age. Reaching into her pocket, she pulled out her phone and quickly composed a text to Danny, who was always reliable when it came to dealing with these kinds of problems.

> Hey Danny, I think we've got rats in the library. Can you come by and check it out when you get a chance?

As she hit send, she glanced around the room, her eyes scanning the towering shelves. She wondered if she might catch a glimpse of the unwelcome intruders. She made a mental note to be extra vigilant in her cleaning, ensuring no crumb would attract them further.

A few moments later, her phone buzzed with Danny's response.

> Sure. Whereabouts?

> Around the bookcase to the left of the fireplace.

There was a brief pause before her phone buzzed again.

> OK.

Karin smiled at his promptness.

> Thanks! x

Karin tucked her phone back in her pocket. The scratching noise had stopped for the moment, but she couldn't shake the uneasy feeling it had left behind. She wondered if the rats had caused any damage to the valuable books or the structure of the shelves.

Determined to continue her work despite the disturbance, she finished cleaning the fireplace, carefully brushing away the last remnants of soot.

A few minutes later, she heard footsteps approaching. Danny, with his usual stony-faced demeanour, entered the library, toolbox in hand. He gave her a reassuring nod before heading straight to the bookcase she had indicated. He inspected the area, his experienced hands moving over the wood, searching for any signs of the unwelcome intruders.

Karin stayed nearby, ready to assist if needed, but also curious about what he might find. The library, normally a place of peace, now felt like it held secrets and perhaps hidden dangers. As Danny worked, she hoped it was just rats and nothing more sinister lurking behind the shelves.

As Ben opened the front door, the familiar creak of the old hinges greeted him. Sally met him in the foyer with a smile and handed him a small stack of post.

"Thanks, Sally," Ben said, taking the letters from her. Duke trotted off towards the kitchen, clearly exhausted from their walk. His tail wagged lazily as he disappeared around the corner.

Ben made his way down the grand hallway, and then entered the library. Inside, he found Karin standing beside Danny, who was kneeling on the floor, inspecting the base of a bookcase. A puzzled expression crossed Ben's face.

The Crimes of Middlemoor Estate

"What are you both doing?" he asked, his curiosity piqued.

Karin turned to him, a look of concern on her face. "I keep hearing scratching noises and now I'm convinced we have rats. Danny's taking a look."

Danny stood up and dusted off his hands. "There are definitely rats within the walls of a house like this, but I can't see an opening. As long as they stay in the walls, we shouldn't have to worry too much."

Just then, Seb entered the room, his ears apparently having caught the tail end of the conversation. "Did I hear someone say rats? Oh, Danny, you must check again! We have to be certain."

Danny sighed, clearly exasperated. "No, Sebastian, I'm not bending down again!"

Before the conversation could continue, Ben's attention was drawn to one of the letters in his hand. His eyes widened as he read it. "Oh my God!" he exclaimed. "I've been offered a place at Cambridge University!"

The room fell silent for a second, then erupted in loud cries of "congratulations". Karin was the first to react, wrapping Ben in a hug. "Ben, that's amazing! Well done!"

Danny clapped him on the back, grinning broadly. "Congratulations, bud! That's fantastic news!"

Seb, not to be outdone, stepped forward and gave Ben an enthusiastic squeeze. "Ah, Ben, you clever boy! How extraordinary! We must celebrate!"

Despite the warm response, Ben's face remained troubled. "Thank you, everyone, but I can't think about this now. Not with Ma and Pa missing. I might have to defer."

Karin placed a reassuring hand on his shoulder. "Hang on, let's not make any rash decisions just yet. We don't know if they're actually missing. Let's wait and see what happens."

Ben nodded slowly. "I guess. I have a few weeks to decide."

"Exactly," Karin said. "So, let's be excited for now." She leaned in and kissed him on the cheek, her positivity a stark contrast to the anxiety everyone had felt over the last few days.

As the group stood in the library, the earlier worry about rats seemed to fade into the background, replaced by the collective celebration of Ben's achievement. The atmosphere in the room felt a little lighter, a little more hopeful, even as the larger mysteries of the estate remained unsolved.

It was 7 p.m., and Ben and Camilla were seated at a wooden table in the Cornish Arms, a popular and beloved pub in the heart of Tavistock. The atmosphere was cosy, with the glow from old-fashioned lanterns and the murmur of flowing conversations. The pub's charm oozed from its rustic decor and the staff's friendly smiles.

As they perused their menus, a waiter approached. "Good evening. Can I get you something to drink?"

Ben's face lit up as he made a decision. "Could we have a bottle of your finest champagne, please?"

"Yes, of course. Any nibbles to start?"

Camilla, glancing at Ben for a brief second, added, "Some olives and bread with dipping oils, please."

Just then, Ben's phone vibrated on the table, its screen

flashing Sally's name. He excused himself politely and stepped outside, where the cool air contrasted sharply with the warmth inside. He rarely answered his phone during company, but given recent events, he knew it could be necessary. Unfortunately, he wasn't wrong.

"Sally, what's up?"

"Ben, I'm so sorry to interrupt your evening." Sally's voice was tense as she continued, "The police want to bring in forensics to search the house. It's serious. They need everyone to move out."

The gravity of the situation hit Ben instantly—he knew he had to get home. "I'll come now. Camilla will understand."

Re-entering the pub, Ben walked back to the table. "Camilla, I'm so sorry. I need to get home. The police are bringing in forensics."

Camilla's fingers tightened slightly around her glass as she masked her own worry. "Go, Ben. It's fine."

"I feel terrible leaving you like this, though."

She shook her head gently. "No, don't be silly. That's way more important. I can ring Rebecca and ask her to come and join me. You go."

"Oh, please do ring Rebecca, it'll make me feel better knowing you're not alone. I'll leave an open tab and sort it tomorrow. Order whatever you like and enjoy for me."

After a moment's pause, Camilla said, "Alright, thank you. Now go and keep me posted. I'm so sorry."

He kissed her softly on the cheek and hurried out of the pub, his mind already racing ahead.

At the estate entrance, Ben was met by police officers whose serious expressions mirrored the tension that had enveloped his home for the past week. The large iron gates, typically a symbol of security and grandeur, seemed foreboding under the harsh glare of the police lights. Ben presented his ID, his hand trembling slightly as he handed it over. One of the officers scrutinised it briefly before nodding and waving him through. As the gates slowly creaked open, Ben couldn't shake the feeling that he was crossing into a realm of uncertainty and fear.

He drove up the long, winding drive at a cautious pace, each turn revealing more police vehicles and uniformed officers spread out across the expansive grounds. The estate, usually a sanctuary of peace and beauty, was heavy with official activity, and the flashing lights cast eerie shapes over the manicured lawns and stately trees. The familiar landscape now seemed distorted.

Two more officers awaited him at the front entrance. Their presence was a stark reminder of the seriousness of the investigation. They stepped forward as he parked; their expressions were professional and gave nothing away. One of them raised a hand to his radio and the device crackled to life.

"Detective Sergeant Ransome, Mr. Ashworth has arrived."

Moments later, DS Ransome appeared from the grand entrance of the mansion. His demeanour was calm yet urgent, his stride purposeful as he approached Ben. "Good evening, Ben," he greeted, his tone laced with a mix of sympathy and determination. "I'm sorry this is happening so quickly, but we need to search the house immediately. Sally has packed a bag for you to stay at hers."

Ben's heart sank and cold dread spread through his chest. "Why? Is something wrong?"

Ransome's eyes met his, serious and unwavering. "We need to rule out anything sinister. Are there blueprints of the house and a map of the land?"

Ben nodded. "There should be blueprints in my father's office. The garden is surrounded by a brick wall containing 60 acres, and beyond that, we have 400 acres of land."

"Alright," Ransome said, his voice steady. "We'll start with the house and gardens. Your parents are now on the missing persons register as a precaution."

A lump formed in Ben's throat. "Why?"

"It will hopefully help us find them quicker. We've created a profile to send across the country."

Ben swallowed hard. "Okay," he managed to say.

DS Ransome placed a reassuring hand on Ben's shoulder. "It's alright, Ben. We'll do everything we can." With that, he turned and headed back inside, leaving Ben standing there, feeling more lost than ever.

Sally walked over, her presence a comforting contrast to the stern police officers. She put her arm around Ben. "Come on, come to mine for some tea. Karin's staying over too."

Ben forced a small smile, grateful for her support. "Where's Sebastian?"

Sally grinned, knowing exactly how to lighten the mood. "Take a guess."

Ben chuckled despite himself. "Danny's?"

"Yes!" Sally laughed, and they both giggled, the momentary lightness a brief respite from the heavy reality.

Ben joined Karin at Sally and Terry's house. The familiar warmth of their home and the presence of friends provided a much-needed sense of normality. As they settled in, Ben's mind raced with thoughts of his parents and the investigation, but he found some solace in the support around him. Their presence was a reminder that he wasn't facing this ordeal alone. The night stretched on, and Ben's thoughts remained troubled, especially knowing that an extensive search was happening right now.

TAVISTOCK HERITAGE & HILLS

Middlemoor Estate Still in Turmoil as Mysterious Disappearance Continues to Grip Family

It feels as though it was only last night that Middlemoor Estate was thrust into pandemonium, with police swarming the grounds. Yet over a month has passed since the sprawling estate, known for its peaceful landscapes and centuries-old history, became the focal point of a dramatic investigation into the baffling and unsettling disappearance of Mr. and Mrs. Ashworth.

The couple, well-known figures in the community, were reported missing by their son, Benedict Ashworth, prompting an immediate and urgent response from law enforcement. The normally quiet estate was transformed into a scene of controlled chaos, with officers and forensic teams conducting what was described as an "all-encompassing" search.

Investigators combed through the property with no breakthrough. Despite extensive efforts, no evidence emerged to suggest where the couple had gone or how they had disappeared. While the police believe a change to the CCTV settings indicates it to be a voluntary departure, no one could understand why they would leave or what they were running from.

And those questions remain. Why did Benedict's parents disappear? Was it truly voluntary, as the CCTV seems to suggest? And if so, why would they leave everything behind?

Despite every effort to uncover the truth, all avenues explored have come to a dead end. The case, though at a standstill, remains open, with authorities stating it will not be actively pursued until new evidence comes to light. The mystery of the Ashworths' disappearance continues to grip the village of Middlemoor, but without fresh leads, the investigation has reached an uncertain pause.

Chapter Ten

Due to the vast expanse of the estate, a full month had passed before Ben, Karin, and Sebastian were finally allowed to return to the house. Unfortunately, the conclusion of the forensic search stemmed from a frustrating lack of findings. Not a single clue emerged to indicate where Ben's parents might be, how they left, or even when they had disappeared.

The investigation into the CCTV system confirmed what had already raised questions: at precisely 11.28 p.m., someone had placed the cameras on the eco setting. While the settings could be adjusted in various locations, this particular change had been made on the house panel: a control point requiring a passcode only Mr. Ashworth knew. Terry, whose alibi placed him with Sally in the gatehouse, was ruled out as a suspect. With no other plausible explanation, the police began to consider the possibility that Mr. and Mrs. Ashworth might have left voluntarily.

Although the police had wrapped up their investigation

inside the house, searches continued in the grounds. This ongoing activity forced Ben to adjust his routine, and he took his runs with Duke through the village instead. As he jogged along familiar paths, he couldn't help but notice a change in Middlemoor. The once-quiet village buzzed with speculation; its residents whispering theories and casting sympathetic glances his way. Nothing like this had ever happened there before, and the mystery surrounding his parents' disappearance had become the village's primary topic of conversation.

Ben tried to ignore the stares and whispered conversations, focusing on the rhythm of his runs and the steady companionship of Duke. But no matter how hard he tried, unanswered questions lingered. Eventually, the search of the gardens came up empty as well, leaving the investigation at a dead end.

Grieving is different for everyone, and Ben's journey through it was fraught with complexity. Struggling to cope with the unknown, his initial shock and sadness soon morphed into a simmering anger. He became increasingly convinced that his parents had orchestrated their disappearance, driven by the so-called "tradition" mentioned in their cryptic letter. To him, it seemed as though they had planned everything meticulously: signing over their assets to vanish and start anew. Ben found it impossible to fathom any other explanation.

Questions swirled relentlessly in his mind: was this truly a tradition, as the letter suggested, or was it a carefully crafted pretext for their sudden departure? Were they somewhere far away, enjoying a new life, while he was left to pick up the pieces? These thoughts gnawed at him, transforming his confusion into a deep-seated resentment. As his anger grew, so did his refusal to discuss his parents. Conversations about them were met with cold silence or a swift change of subject. It was his way of dealing with the grief, shutting out the pain by severing any emotional ties. Sad as it was, it was the only way he knew to protect himself, and no one could argue with his method of coping.

Amidst this emotional turmoil, one silver lining emerged: Camilla's unwavering support. Her presence became a constant source of comfort, and over time, their close friendship blossomed into a romantic relationship. This newfound connection brought a ray of hope into Ben's otherwise dark days. Their relationship remained a well-guarded secret, though, known only to them and Ben's trusted staff. Given Camilla's split from Richard, they were cautious about public appearances, mindful of the delicate social dynamics and the unspoken "bro code" that governed their circle. Camilla often joined Ben and his staff for dinner. She was much loved by them all.

Ben and Richard strolled onto the lush fairway. Ben adjusted his glove, squinting to locate the distant flag, while Richard fished a golf ball out of his bag, a casual smile playing on his lips.

"So, how's life treating you these days?" Richard asked as he lined up his shot. His posture was relaxed, his confidence apparent as he swung the club. The ball sailed through the air with a satisfying thwack, landing just shy of the green. Richard watched it with a self-assured grin, as if everything in his life would land just as neatly.

Ben observed the ball's trajectory, forcing himself to maintain a neutral expression despite the unease gnawing at him. "Not too bad, can't complain. How about you?" he responded, though his thoughts were miles away.

"Well, my father sat me down last night and basically said I'm on thin ice with him—apparently one step away from being kicked out. Honestly, though, he's threatened it so many times before. It'll never happen. It's all talk." Richard laughed, the sound more dismissive than amused.

Ben's expression tightened. "It's not the drugs again, is it? Why are you doing this to yourself?"

Richard brushed him off with a careless shrug. "It's called having a good time. I'll grow out of it one day, trust me. Just enjoying life at the moment." He flashed a smile at Ben, as if expecting his friend to join in with the joke.

"Yeah," Ben said slowly, the weight of his words hanging in the air, "sounds really fun…"

A heavy silence settled between them. Ben turned his gaze onto the course, pretending to focus on his next move, but his mind was elsewhere. He knew Richard too well to believe the bravado, the hollow ring of his laughter echoing in Ben's ears long after it faded.

Richard planted his club onto the ground and leaned on it. "Actually, there's something I've been meaning to tell you." He paused for effect, a sparkle in his eyes. "I've decided I'm going to try to win Camilla back."

Ben's heart skipped a beat, but he kept his face neutral. "Oh? I didn't know you two were still in touch."

"We're not," Richard admitted, picking up his tee. "But I can't stop thinking about her. You know how it is, right? When someone just gets under your skin and you can't shake them off?"

Ben nodded slowly, a tight smile on his face. "Yeah, I get it."

Richard swung his club in a practised arc, lost in thought. "I've been thinking about what went wrong, what I could have done differently. I think I still have a chance, you know. If I can just get her to see how much I've changed, maybe we can start over."

Ben's grip tightened on his club. "People do change," he said carefully, "but sometimes things happen for a reason."

Richard looked at him, curiosity in his eyes. "What about you, Ben? Anyone special in your life?"

Ben hesitated, his mind racing. "I've been... seeing someone. It's still new."

"Good for you, man," Richard said sincerely. "You deserve to be happy. I just hope I can have the same luck with Camilla."

Ben forced a laugh, stepping up to take his shot. "Yeah, who knows what the future holds?"

Richard leaned on his club, watching Ben prepare for his next shot. "You know, maybe you could help me out," he said, a hopeful tone in his voice.

Ben paused. "Help you out? How do you mean?"

"Well," Richard began, choosing his words carefully, "maybe you could talk to Camilla for me. Just feel things out, see where her head's at. You're close to her, right?"

Ben's heart was racing. He cleared his throat, trying to stay composed. "Uh, yeah, we've talked a bit. But I'm not sure I should get involved. These things can get complicated."

Richard sighed, frustration edging into his voice. "I know, but I'm at a loss here, Ben. I just want to know if there's any chance for us. It would mean a lot if you could just... you know, put in a good word."

Ben looked down the fairway, his mind churning. "I'll see what I can do," he said finally, his voice measured. "But I can't promise anything."

Richard's face lit up with a grateful smile. "That's all I'm asking for. Thanks, Ben. You're a real friend."

Ben nodded, forcing a smile as he took his shot. The ball flew true, landing on the green. As they walked towards the next hole, Ben couldn't shake the unease settling in his stomach.

Richard, oblivious, chatted happily about his plans, his excitement clear. Ben listened, nodding in the right places, all the while wondering how he was going to navigate this delicate situation without hurting someone he cared about.

As they reached the green, Ben's thoughts raced. He knew there was no way he could help Richard without compromising his own relationship with Camilla. They were already too far into something real, something he couldn't and didn't want to back away from.

"Look, Richard," Ben started, trying to choose his words carefully, "I don't think I can help you with Camilla. It's... it's complicated."

Richard looked puzzled, his smile fading slightly. "What do you mean? I thought you two were friends."

"We are," Ben said quickly, feeling the pressure of the situation mounting. "But sometimes, getting involved in other people's relationships isn't a good idea. I wouldn't want to make things worse for you."

Richard frowned, considering Ben's words. "I get that, but I really thought you could just talk to her. It wouldn't have to be a big deal."

Ben felt a pang of guilt. He wanted to be honest with Richard, to tell him everything, but he knew it would only complicate things further. "I'm sorry, Richard. I just... I can't."

Richard sighed, frustration evident in his expression. "I understand. I guess I just have to figure this out on my own."

Ben nodded, relieved but conflicted. "Yeah, sometimes that's the best way."

They continued their game in strained silence, the easy camaraderie from earlier replaced by an unspoken tension. Ben knew his friendship with Richard was on shaky ground, but he also knew his relationship with Camilla was worth protecting, even if it meant keeping a secret.

Ben walked into his father's office, the familiar scent of polished wood bringing a wave of bittersweet memories. He approached the large oak desk, and his eyes briefly glanced over the papers and family photographs scattered across its surface. Taking a deep breath, he reached for the phone and dialled a number.

"You're through to the Cambridge University switchboard. May I ask what the call is regarding?" The operator's voice was polite but distant.

"It's for admissions," Ben replied, his voice steady.

"Thank you. Please hold while I transfer you."

The line went quiet. There was no soothing hold music, just deafening silence and the sound of Ben's heart thudding in his chest, each beat a reminder of the gravity of his decision.

"Good afternoon, you're through to admissions. How can I help you?" The new voice was welcoming, but it heightened Ben's anxiety.

"Hello, my name is Benedict Ashworth," he began. "I would like to withdraw my application. I've been accepted, but my circumstances have changed, and I'm no longer able to attend."

There was a brief pause before the admissions officer responded. "Is there any reason? We have many options that might work for you."

Ben closed his eyes, grappling with the complexity of his situation. "No, it's very complicated. I need to stay at home for now."

The voice on the other end softened. "Would you like me to add you to the defer list? That way, if things change, we can hold your place for up to a year after acceptance, like a gap year."

Relief washed over Ben. "Actually, yes please. I didn't know that was an option."

"Of course," the admissions officer replied. "Let me take your full name and application number, and I'll get that sorted for you."

Ben provided the details, feeling a strange mix of sadness and hope. "Thank you so much," he said, meaning every word.

After hanging up, Ben stood for a moment in the quiet of

his father's office. Despite the uncertainty of the future, he felt a small sense of peace knowing that Cambridge would still be there, waiting for him, whenever he was ready to move forward. After all, he was now the sole owner of W&A, and he wouldn't let his grandfather down. The responsibility was overwhelming, but Benedict embraced it with determination.

TAVISTOCK HERITAGE & HILLS

Middlemoor Estate Finally Has Reason to Celebrate After Years of Turmoil

Middlemoor Estate was celebrating this weekend as Benedict Ashworth married his long-term girlfriend, Camilla Stobbs. The prestigious estate has had its share of upset following the mysterious disappearance of Benedict's parents several years ago. The intimate wedding that took place in Santorini will have been a welcome respite from the speculation and worry that has hung over Middlemoor Estate.

Benedict has run the estate since inheriting it on his 18_{th} birthday, and he turned down his placement at Cambridge University to take up his parents' bequest. Camilla, who previously worked as a youth programme coordinator at the local community centre, joined her now husband in the family business 5 years ago following its expansion.

Controversy followed the Ashworths and their ceremony didn't go smoothly thanks to the presence of Richard Coldwell. Rumours have circulated that the well-known heir to the Coldwell biscuit empire has been battling with drugs, and this seemed to be confirmed at the wedding. Guests have reported that his behaviour was erratic and he seemed bitter that his best friend was marrying his ex-girlfriend.

For now, at least, talk of the Middlemoor mystery has been replaced with conversations about the wedding. Let's hope this heralds a more peaceful and happier future for the troubled estate.

Part Two

Camilla

Chapter Eleven

Ben, Camilla, and Keith had been in Plymouth, inspecting a construction site slated to house new offices. Ben, committed to fostering strong community relations, always insisted on meeting with local businesses to address questions and concerns directly before any project commenced. Today's meeting was unusually brief, with no significant issues raised, allowing them to return home earlier than anticipated. They arrived just in time to welcome Camilla's mother, Caroline, who hadn't been expecting to see them until later. She was visiting for a few weeks. They had seen each other infrequently since Caroline moved to Penzance a few years ago, making these moments all the more precious.

"Hi, Mum, how are you? Did you have a safe journey?" Camilla embraced her mother tightly, her excitement evident in her voice.

"I did. And thank you for sending the car," Caroline replied.

"That's okay! I'm glad you're here. I've missed you so much."

"Oh, sweetie, I always miss you too." They hugged again, savouring the moment after their time apart. Ben entered the hallway, his presence adding to the joy of the reunion.

"Well, hello, my favourite mother-in-law. How are you?" He kissed her on the cheek with genuine affection.

"Oh, you have to say that, I'm your only mother-in-law!" Caroline laughed, her eyes twinkling with joy. "But yes, I'm well, thank you. How have you been?"

"I'm well too, thanks. Just heading out with the dogs for a walk, then I've got a dentist appointment. I'll be back around 5 p.m., and we can catch up properly then." Ben kissed Caroline on the cheek again, gave Camilla a quick kiss, and went to the kitchen, calling for Duke and Sibel. The dogs bounded towards him, tails wagging excitedly.

"I'll take the bags!" Sebastian sang as he waltzed down the staircase.

"Oh, Sebastian, I need you in my life every day!" Caroline exclaimed, giving him a big squeeze. "You're such a delight!"

"You flatter me, Caroline." Sebastian grinned, picking up the luggage with ease. "I'll put these in your room."

"Perhaps we can head into Tavistock for a little mooch later?" Camilla suggested.

"That sounds perfect," Caroline agreed.

As Sebastian carried the bags upstairs, Camilla and Caroline moved into the drawing room. They sat on the plush sofa and Camilla poured them both a cup of tea; the aroma filled the air.

"How's Penzance been?" Camilla asked, genuinely interested in her mother's life.

"It's been lovely, but I do wish we could see each other more often." Caroline's eyes misted slightly. "I miss our daily chats and walks."

"I miss them too, Mum. But we'll make the most of your stay, for sure!" Camilla squeezed her mother's hand.

They chatted for a while longer, sharing stories and laughter, the bond between them as strong as ever. Finally, Camilla looked at the clock and said, "Shall we head out to Tavistock now? I know a great little café that just opened."

"Yes, let's do that," Caroline said, standing up. "I'm looking forward to it."

As they gathered their things and headed out, Camilla felt a deep sense of contentment. This visit was just what they both needed—a chance to reconnect and create new memories together.

After a leisurely stroll around the village, where they enjoyed browsing in cute shops and picking up a few delightful items, Camilla and Caroline decided to relax with a coffee at Pip's Coffee House. The atmosphere was delightful, and they spent a pleasant hour chatting and people-watching. Once they felt rejuvenated, they made their way back to Middlemoor Estate, enjoying the scenic drive through the countryside. Upon their return, Seb welcomed them at the door, offering glasses of rich red wine.

"Here you go, ladies. Tonight we're having braised beef with creamy mash, tender stem broccoli, and a red wine jus. What's that? Too much red wine? Never, darlings!" he announced with a flourish, placing their shopping bags on a nearby table before sashaying off down the corridor.

"Oh, Camilla, where did you find Sebastian? I'm obsessed!" Caroline laughed, her eyes sparkling with amusement.

"Don't, I'm convinced this place would crumble without him. Everyone needs a Sebastian!" Camilla chuckled.

As they entered the kitchen, the rich aroma of slow-cooked beef filled the air. "Oh, Sally, the beef smells absolutely gorgeous," Caroline exclaimed, her mouth watering.

"Only my best dish for the best people! How are you, Caroline?" she asked, enveloping Caroline in a hug.

"All the better for being here!" Caroline beamed, feeling the genuine warmth that made Middlemoor Estate so special.

"Is Ben back yet?" Camilla asked Seb, glancing around for any sign of her husband.

"No, I haven't seen him or the dogs. He must have taken them with him," Seb replied, shaking his head.

"Hmm." Camilla checked the ornate clock on the kitchen wall. It read 5.45 p.m. She pulled out her phone. "I'll try calling him," she said, more to herself than anyone else. "Straight to voicemail." She frowned.

"Dinner is practically done, Camilla. Would you like me to hold off and wait for Ben? He can't be much longer, surely?" Sally asked, concern creasing her forehead.

"No, it's okay, Sally. Mum's had a long day, so we'll start," Camilla decided, trying to sound more confident than she felt.

"Of course." Sally nodded. "Would everyone head to the dining room? I'll bring it through."

As they moved towards the dining room, Seb cheerfully took charge, guiding them to their seats with passion. The room was elegantly set, with candles flickering gently and soft music playing in the background. Karin topped everyone's drinks up. Camilla couldn't help but feel a pang of worry about Ben's absence but pushed it aside, focusing on the comfort of the moment.

Sally soon appeared with a platter of beautifully arranged food. "Here we are, ladies. Enjoy!" she said, placing the dishes on the table with care.

As they savoured the locally sourced braised beef and engaged in lively conversation, the evening took a sudden, chilling turn. They heard furious barking and a rush of paws at the back door. Camilla's heart skipped a beat. She sprang to her feet and peered through the window.

"It's Duke and Sibel!" she exclaimed. She hurried to let them in. The dogs were cold and panting heavily, their fur damp from the night air. Camilla stepped outside, the darkness enveloping her. "Ben!" she called out, her voice trembling. The only response was the distant chorus of nocturnal creatures. "Ben!" Her heart raced and tears welled up in her eyes. "Something's not right!" Panic surged through her as she grabbed a coat and the keys to the golf buggy.

"Where are you going?" her mother asked, alarmed.

"Something's not right. I have to go look," Camilla insisted, her voice breaking.

"I'm coming with you!" Danny shouted, already following her out the door.

They jumped into the buggy, its headlights cutting a narrow path through the dense darkness. Danny clung to the side as Camilla drove recklessly, her voice hoarse from shouting Ben's name into the night. After a frantic five-minute search, Camilla abruptly stopped and jumped out.

"Ben? Please answer me!" she cried, her voice echoing in the stillness.

"Camilla, come on. We need to head back to the house. We need to call the police. He could be hurt," Danny urged, his own fear palpable.

The police arrived swiftly, their faces grim as they registered the familiar address—another missing person from the same house, the same family. Reinforcements soon followed, scouring the gardens with flashlights and sniffer dogs. Camilla watched, her heart heavy with dread. The search continued through the night, stretching into the cold, unforgiving dawn. Exhausted and emotionally drained, she finally collapsed on the library sofa.

The following day, Camilla entered the kitchen, her eyes red and swollen from sleeplessness and worry "What's going on?" Camilla asked, seeing Seb and DS Ransome deep in conversation.

"Benedict didn't attend his dentist appointment, so I'm placing him on the missing persons list immediately. We need all hands on deck for this. I'm so sorry, Camilla. Please be assured we are working as quickly as possible to find him," Ransome said, his tone firm but compassionate. He left the room with purposeful strides.

"Wait, Seb, what's he suggesting? How does he know

Ben didn't go to the dentist?" Camilla's voice wavered, a mix of confusion and rising panic.

"There was a voicemail from the dentist, but I didn't get it until 8 a.m. this morning. I went straight to Detective Sergeant Ransome. I'm so sorry, Camilla." Seb's voice cracked, and tears streamed down his face as he wrapped his arms around her. Camilla stood still in shock, supporting Seb with one hand while staring blankly into space. She felt numb. Where on earth could Ben be?

Meanwhile, Ransome coordinated the search from the estate's security office, his eyes fixed on the screens displaying footage of the grounds. The knowledge that Ben had not kept his appointment and the return of the dogs without him suggested he was still somewhere on the property. Terry replayed the footage from the previous afternoon, showing Ben, Duke, and Sibel exiting the back door. Ben paused to adjust his coat, then walked off into the garden, the dogs bounding ahead. The cameras, limited in their coverage, captured Ben disappearing into the shadows of the estate.

Ransome leaned closer, his eyes narrowing. "Rewind that. Play it again," he instructed, his pulse quickening.

Terry complied. They scrutinised every detail, searching for any clue, any sign that might explain Ben's sudden disappearance. The cameras revealed nothing beyond Ben's last known steps.

"Damn it, we need more coverage of the grounds," Ransome muttered, frustration evident in his voice. "Expand the search perimeter. We have to find him."

Ben was out there somewhere, and time was running out.

Camilla sat alone in the dimly lit library, the once comforting room now a cage of torment. The persistent scratching of rats behind the walls was a faint backdrop to her overwhelming worry, though she barely registered the sound. Her mind raced, desperately trying to piece together where Ben could be.

The door creaked open and Sally entered, followed by Karin. Sally carried a tray of tea, the porcelain cups clinking softly, while Karin held a plate of pastries. They placed them gently on the table, their movements careful and quiet, as if not to disturb the fragile silence. Camilla couldn't even think about food, her stomach was so knotted with anxiety, but she managed a weak smile and thanked them.

They all sat in silence, the air thick with unspoken fears. Caroline joined them shortly after.

"Good morning, all," Caroline greeted softly, sitting next to Camilla. She put her arm around Camilla and pulled her into a hug.

The dam of Camilla's composure broke, and she began to sob uncontrollably. The sound of her tears, raw and heart-wrenching, echoed through the room. It was a sound that spoke of helplessness and profound loss, shattering the stoic facade they had all been trying to maintain.

Sally's eyes welled up, her usual steadfast demeanour crumpling as she reached out to squeeze Camilla's hand. Karin bit her lip, tears streaming down her cheeks, while Caroline held Camilla tighter, her own tears flowing freely.

The Crimes of Middlemoor Estate

The room was filled with the collective sorrow of friends who could do nothing but share in the grief and fear of the unknown.

Time seemed to stretch endlessly. Every minute that passed without news of Ben felt like an eternity. The sound of dogs barking in the distance was the only indication that the search was still ongoing, a thin thread of hope in the overwhelming darkness.

Camilla's mind wandered to every possible scenario, each more terrifying than the last. She thought of Ben, out there alone, possibly hurt or worse. The uncertainty was unbearable. Her heart ached with a pain she had never known, a gnawing emptiness that consumed her.

As the hours dragged on, the library became a silent sanctuary of shared sorrow. The untouched tea grew cold, and the pastries remained uneaten. Camilla felt a deep gratitude for their presence, knowing that she was not alone in her grief.

But nothing could soothe the agony of not knowing. As day turned into night, and the search continued, the fear that Ben might never return grew stronger. Camilla clung to the hope that he would be found safe, but the leverage of those hours passed made that hope feel more like a fragile whisper in the storm of her despair.

TAVISTOCK HERITAGE & HILLS

Heiress or Harlot? The Mystery Deepens as Middlemoor Estate is Plagued by Another Disappearance

When Benedict Ashworth vanished without a trace, Middlemoor Estate was once again thrown into despair. The locals rallied at first, but the disappearance quickly sparked rumours, especially with this being the second tragic mystery to strike the Ashworth family. Now, suspicion has shifted towards Benedict's wife, Camilla, whose presence in the close-knit community has become a source of relentless gossip and scrutiny. Though her marriage ties her to Middlemoor, Camilla's outsider origins have fuelled theories that she had ulterior motives in joining the Ashworth family—and, perhaps, in hastening their downfall.

As news of Benedict's disappearance spread, Camilla's every move was under a microscope. Some villagers have taken to calling her names like "gold-digger" and "black widow", while others eagerly feed on any hint of scandal. Although a handful still offer her genuine sympathy, the majority seem to mask their curiosity with false concern.

Despite these accusations, Camilla remains resolute in her search for Ben. Each venture into Tavistock is a painful reminder of the community's doubts: close friends have distanced themselves, acquaintances have grown cold, and even shopkeepers eye her with suspicion. At home, Middlemoor Estate has begun to show signs of neglect. Gardens once vibrant with life grow wild, their blooms wilting. The once-warm halls lie quiet and deserted, echoing only memories of a happier past.

We spoke to local residents and the consensus seems to be that Camilla has something to do with Ben's disappearance. One villager, who didn't want to be named, said, "Did you hear? She's after the estate. Poor Ben, I wonder what really happened." Another told us, "I wouldn't be surprised if she was involved."

Yet, despite her distress and the rumours, Camilla refuses to give up hope. She has thrown herself into the search for Ben, reviewing his belongings, retracing his steps, and hiring new investigators in her bid for answers. It has taken a toll on her health; sleepless nights have left her gaunt, her once-bright eyes shadowed with exhaustion. But her love for Ben drives her on, even as the world around her closes in.

Chapter Twelve

DS Ransome reviewed the footage of Ben's last known movements for what felt like the hundredth time. Suddenly, something caught his eye. A subtle detail he had previously overlooked—a glint of light in the distance, just as Ben disappeared from view. He paused the video, and leaned towards the screen to get a closer look. Could it be a reflection? A hidden structure? He had to investigate further.

The following morning, he gathered a team and returned to the spot where Ben was last seen. They spread out, meticulously combing the area for any clue that might explain what had caught the light. Hours passed, and just as they were about to give up, one of the officers shouted, "Over here!"

They had stumbled upon an almost invisible structure, concealed beneath a thick layer of ivy and tangled roots, nestled between two large Devonshire stone boulders that had long ago settled into the earth. The entrance to what appeared to be an underground war bunker was so well hidden it had escaped the notice of Danny and previous gardeners for years. A sense of anticipation hung in the air as they prepared to enter, carefully cutting away the foliage that had kept it secret from the world.

Camilla, her mother, and the staff watched from a distance as the police presence at Middlemoor Estate intensified. This could be the breakthrough they had been desperately seeking.

As Ransome led the way into the dark narrow tunnel, he couldn't shake the feeling they were on the verge of uncovering something significant. The tunnel walls were damp and cold, the air thick with the scent of earth and decay. They moved slowly, carefully, their flashlights cutting through the darkness.

Finally, after what felt like an eternity, they reached the end of the tunnelled room. Ransome's shoulders slumped as he realised their worst fear: Ben was not here. Just a very well-preserved memory of war time. The bunker had yielded nothing but dust and echoes of history.

Ransome called for a final sweep of the bunker, instructing his team to leave no stone unturned. The officers moved methodically, their flashlights sweeping through the dim, musty air. Every corner, every crevice was meticulously searched, but it was futile. The place was deserted, a relic of a bygone era, long forgotten by time. With a heavy heart, Ransome knew he had to make the difficult call to end the search on the estate grounds. There were no other leads to follow, no other corners to explore. Continuing without direction would be a waste of resources and would only prolong the agony of those waiting for answers.

Camilla stood at the entrance, her face a mask of anxiety and fragile hope. As she saw the officers' expressions, her heart sank, a cold dread creeping into her chest. The grim faces told her everything she needed to know before Ransome even spoke.

"I'm sorry, Mrs. Ashworth," Ransome said gently, his voice filled with compassion. "The bunker is empty. There's no sign of Ben."

The words struck Camilla like a physical blow. She staggered slightly, gripping a nearby tree trunk for support. The police had hoped this bunker would be the breakthrough they needed, the place where they might finally find Ben and bring some solace to his family and the staff. Instead, they were left with more questions and a growing sense of despair.

The search of Middlemoor's grounds had been exhaustive. Over the past weeks, every inch of the estate had been meticulously combed, from the sprawling gardens with their intricate hedge mazes to the dense, shadowy woodlands that bordered the property. Teams of officers had sifted through the underbrush, scanned the ponds and streams, and even climbed into the old crumbling attics of the estate's outbuildings. They had interviewed staff, neighbours, and anyone who might have seen or heard something unusual. Despite their relentless efforts, they had found no trace of Ben.

As DS Ransome delivered the devastating news,

Camilla's eyes filled with tears. She struggled to maintain her composure, her mind reeling. She had clung to the hope that Ben would be found, that this nightmare would finally come to an end. Now, that hope was slipping through her fingers, leaving her with a void of despair and uncertainty.

"The search of Middlemoor grounds has come to a close," Ransome announced to everyone gathered. "We've covered every possible area extensively. Without new leads, there's nothing more we can do here."

Camilla nodded, her mind numb. She understood the reality, but it didn't make it any easier to accept. She thanked the officers for their efforts, though the words felt hollow and inadequate. She watched as the police packed up their equipment, their movements slow and pensive. The chatter and noise of the investigation faded, replaced by a heavy, oppressive silence that settled over Middlemoor.

As the last police vehicle drove away, Camilla stood alone at the entrance of the estate. The staff moved quietly through their duties; their faces emotionless. The vibrant life of the estate had dimmed. Days turned into weeks, each one a relentless march of sorrow and frustration. The villagers, once a close-knit community, seemed to turn inward, their whispers and speculations growing more fervent. Camilla avoided their prying eyes, the gossip and innuendo adding to her torment.

Late at night, in the quiet hours when the rest of the house slept, Camilla wandered the halls. She visited Ben's office, his favourite chair by the fireplace, the library where they had spent so many evenings together. Each empty room was a stark reminder of him.

Her once vibrant spirit was now a shadow of its former self, dulled by the relentless worry and heartache. Yet, even in her darkest moments, a flicker of hope remained. She clung to the belief that somewhere, somehow, Ben was waiting to be found. That hope, fragile as it was, kept her moving forward, kept her searching, even when the world around her seemed determined to give up.

Camilla's resolve hardened into steel. She would not let Middlemoor's secrets remain buried. She would uncover the truth, no matter the cost. And she would bring Ben home.

A week had passed since the final police investigation of the property, and things had settled into an uneasy calm. The officers had been working silently behind closed doors, but nothing had come to light.

Camilla had dozed off in the drawing room, her phone resting beside her. The sharp ring of the doorbell jolted her awake. Groggy, she reached for her phone and noticed a message from Terry:

> Heads up, Richard's on his way over.

Camilla sighed, rubbing her eyes as she rose from the sofa, still feeling exhausted. She shuffled into the hallway, but before she could reach the door, she saw that Seb had already answered it.

"Hello, Richard. What brings you here?" Seb's tone was polite, but there was a cold edge to his words.

"Good afternoon, Sebastian," Richard replied with a forced smile, holding out a small tin. "I brought some shortbread for Camilla and wanted to express my deepest condolences for Ben's disappearance."

Camilla lingered in the shadows, out of Richard's sight, her heart sinking at the mention of Ben.

Seb glanced at the tin, recognising the familiar label of Richard's family's shortbread.

"How thoughtful of you," he said, taking the tin with barely concealed disdain. "I'll make sure she gets them."

"Is she not home? I was hoping to speak with her," Richard asked, peering past Seb as if expecting Camilla to appear.

Seb shot a quick glance towards Camilla, who subtly shook her head, signalling her reluctance to face Richard.

"Unfortunately, she's not," Seb lied smoothly.

Richard frowned, glancing at Camilla's car parked outside. "But her car is here..."

"She took a taxi earlier. Now, if you'll excuse me, I must be going. Goodbye, Richard." Seb's smile didn't reach his eyes as he firmly closed the door, cutting off any further conversation.

Seb turned to Camilla, who was leaning against the wall, her arms crossed tightly over her chest. The strain of the past few days was carved on her face, and the unexpected visit had clearly rattled her.

The doorbell rang again, startling them both. Camilla quickly ducked out of sight as Seb strode over to answer it.

"Oh, hello again!" Seb greeted him with a forced smile.

"Hi, yes, well, there was something else I needed to talk to you about. Long story short, I've been kicked out. My own father has turned his back on me," Richard declared, his voice quivering with manufactured sorrow. "If only he could see what my mother always saw in me. I'm such an incredible person—I only ever wanted the best for them," he lamented, his attempt to summon a tear falling pitifully short. "So, do you think I could stay here?"

"Oh, absolutely not!" Seb blurted out, recoiling in disgust before catching himself. Richard's face registered shock. "I mean, unfortunately, that won't be possible, not with everything that's going on," Seb quickly corrected, plastering on another fake smile.

"Well, I was hoping to ask Camilla, since it's her house," Richard said with an awkward laugh.

"That won't be necessary," Seb shot back smoothly. "I make those decisions as I'm in charge of the estate." He lied without missing a beat.

Camilla, still hiding, stifled a giggle.

"Anyway, must dash. Catch up soon. Bye, Richard," Seb said hastily, shutting the door before Richard could respond again. He turned to Camilla, a bead of sweat forming on his brow.

"He's the last person I wanted to see," she muttered, her voice trembling slightly as she met Seb's concerned gaze.

Her eyes flicked to the tin of shortbread in Seb's hands, her distaste evident. "What are we going to do with those?" she asked, almost as if the very sight of them offended her.

Seb lifted the tin slightly, inspecting it with a raised eyebrow. "I doubt you'll want to keep them," he said, reading her thoughts. "Shall I share them with the others? Or maybe I should just toss them out?"

"I definitely don't want them," Camilla replied quickly, wrinkling her nose in disgust. "He can keep his so-called apology. Go ahead and give them to the others if you think they'll like them."

Seb chuckled softly, setting the tin down on the side table

The Crimes of Middlemoor Estate

with a dismissive wave. "I think I'll pass on that, too. Too many calories for me. But I'll make sure the others know it's up for grabs—if anyone's brave enough to eat them, that is."

Camilla managed a weak smile, appreciating Seb's attempt to lighten the mood. "You always know how to make me feel better," she said, her voice softening with gratitude.

Seb smiled at her. "It's what I'm here for," he said. "Now, why don't you let me run you a nice bubble bath? A long soak will do you some good. I'll even bring you up a margarita."

Camilla's eyes brightened at the suggestion, the tension in her shoulders easing just a bit. "That sounds perfect, Seb. You really are the best."

"Anything for you, Camilla," Seb replied, his tone filled with sincerity. "You go upstairs and relax. I'll take care of everything."

As Camilla turned and went up the stairs, Seb watched her go, his expression softening further. He knew how much she was struggling with Ben's disappearance and the overwhelming emotions of the search ending. Richard's unwelcome visit had only added to her distress, but Seb was determined to shield her from as much as he could.

With a sigh, he picked up the tin of shortbread, staring at it for a moment before setting it back down with a decisive thud. Whatever happened next, he would be there for Camilla, ensuring she had the support she needed—starting with that bubble bath and a perfectly mixed margarita.

As Richard was leaving, he noticed Karin walking up the side of the house, her steps light and unhurried. He couldn't resist; he flashed her a grin and called out, "Well, if it isn't the most beautiful thing I've seen all week."

Karin looked up, surprised, then blushed. She'd always had a soft spot for Richard, though his confidence often threw her off balance. "Richard," she replied, smiling as she approached, "it's been too long. How've you been?"

He leaned back against the house, hands in his pockets, giving her a look that was half smirk, half dare. "Oh, you know me, never better," he said, his tone casual and cocky, though it rang hollow given how he really was feeling.

"How are you holding up?" he asked gently.

Karin sighed, her gaze distant. "Just getting through each day, really. It's been so hard without Ben. We're all feeling his absence."

Richard nodded with faux sincerity. "I can only imagine. Ben and I haven't been close in a while, but I've been thinking about him too. I'm really sorry for what you're going through. I dropped by with some shortbread, and if there's anything I can do, please don't hesitate to reach out."

"Thank you, Richard. That's so kind of you." Her voice dropped. "Anyway, I should be going. Got some sheets to take to the dry cleaners."

"Sheets to the dry cleaners?" he teased, trying to lighten the mood. "With your skills, surely you can handle that yourself?"

She chuckled, the sound momentarily easing the sadness in her eyes. "Normally, yes, but these are velvet with embroidered owls all over them. They came from the Scottish Owl Centre in Whitburn years ago, so they're sentimental. Caroline loves them when she stays, so better safe than sorry."

"Ah, Caroline was staying with you?" he asked, his tone softening. "How's she doing?"

"She's still here, with us until Wednesday morning, but staying in Camilla's room with her. She's taking it hard too... It's been tough on everyone." Karin paused, gathering herself. "I'm just trying to keep busy with the little things, like freshening up the house. Hence the dry-cleaning errand." She gave a faint smile.

Richard smiled back. "You're doing great, keeping yourself occupied. Do you need a lift into the village?"

Her face brightened. "Oh, that would be wonderful, thank you."

"Perfect." He unlocked the car with a click. "Hop in."

Chapter Thirteen

Wednesday morning soon came around. As the taxi pulled up to the house, Caroline's heart twisted. She hadn't wanted this moment to come—not with Ben still missing and everything so unsettled at Middlemoor. But Camilla, stubborn as ever, had insisted she return home. She didn't want her mother feeling trapped at the estate, tangled up in the whispers and threats that had begun to swirl in the local community.

"Camilla, you don't have to stay here," Caroline said softly, a trace of pleading in her voice. "You don't need to be in the middle of this. Come back with me—just until things settle down."

Camilla shook her head and managed a brave smile. "Middlemoor's my home, Mum. I can't just walk away from it. I need to be here in case Ben comes back. Besides, I don't want you here where things could get... difficult."

Caroline reached out and smoothed a stray hair from Camilla's face. "You've always been strong," she whispered.

"Stubborn, too. But promise me you'll look after yourself. Don't take on more than you can bear."

Camilla gripped her mother's hand tightly, her gaze steady. "I'll be fine, Mum. I'll keep you posted, alright?"

Caroline nodded, her heart aching with love and pride. She pulled her daughter into a fierce embrace, holding on as if she could shield her from everything. "You take care of yourself, darling. And don't ever think you have to handle it all alone."

When she finally pulled back, her eyes were damp, and she quickly brushed away a tear. "I love you, Camilla. Remember that."

"I love you too, Mum," Camilla replied, her voice catching slightly.

Caroline got into the taxi, her gaze never leaving Camilla's face as the car began to pull away. She pressed her hand against the glass, watching her daughter grow smaller with each passing second, a lone figure against the vastness of Middlemoor. She kept her eyes on Camilla until the house and her resolute daughter disappeared from view.

Moments later, another car buzzed at the gate. Terry, always vigilant, turned it away with practised ease. Benedict must have pre-arranged a taxi for his mother-in-law, ever the meticulous planner, always one step ahead. His foresight was a small reminder in these tumultuous times.

A few days later, evening fell and Danny gathered everyone in the library for an announcement. His demeanour was sombre as he shared news of his impending departure. His father's health had deteriorated significantly and as Danny had no other family, the responsibility of care fell solely on his shoulders. Camilla, ever the supportive friend and employer, offered to bring his father to the estate, but Danny declined gently. His father's treatment required proximity to a hospital, something Middlemoor couldn't provide.

"Oh, Danny, I hate to see you go but you have to do this. Please know there will always be a place for you at Middlemoor should you wish to come back. I really hope your father's okay. He's welcome to come live here if things improve," Camilla said.

Danny's eyes were filled with gratitude and sorrow. "I feel awful to be leaving now, especially with Ben missing, but I know I must go back home to help him. I don't know how much longer he has. I'm so sorry."

"Please, don't be sorry. That's the last thing you should be saying. You must do what you have to do to support your family. We're your family too, and we are supporting you to go be with your father," Camilla reassured him, her tone firm yet compassionate.

"Thanks, Camilla. I'll pack up now and head out as soon as I can. I'll keep in touch. Come here, Seb, let's have a hug. You know I'm not much of a hugger, but today I'll make an exception."

Seb sprang up from his seat, his face already crumpling, and threw his arms around his friend. His sobs shook his body, and he buried his face into Danny's shoulder, clinging to him as if letting go would make everything fall apart. After a moment, Seb pulled back slightly, his eyes red and glistening with tears, and he managed to crack a small smile. "Who am I going to ogle over now while I'm sipping my morning tea?" he choked out, his voice trembling with his attempt at humour.

Danny let out a soft, shaky laugh, feeling a lump rise in his own throat as he wiped away a tear. "You'll just have to settle for someone else," he replied, trying to keep the mood light. He paused, his eyes growing serious again as he looked between them all. "You've got to promise me you'll keep me posted on Ben. I need to know how he's doing—whatever happens."

"Of course, Danny," Sally said, stepping closer to rub his arm. Her voice was calm but laden with everything left unsaid. "We'll let you know as soon as we hear anything."

Danny nodded, grateful for the support. The reality of leaving them behind, of facing whatever came next on his own, was starting to sink in, but he forced himself to smile at Seb, who was still wiping his eyes. "Take care of yourself, alright? And don't let that tea get cold."

Seb managed a small laugh, even as tears streamed down his face. "I'll try, Danny. You take care, too. We'll miss you."

"Same here," Danny replied softly, giving Seb one last squeeze before letting go. "Same here. I just want to say thank you to everyone for everything you've done. My time at Middlemoor has been the best of my life, and I'll always cherish the memories we've made together. I'll miss the relaxed work life and the place I've been so proud to call home—it's not often you find colleagues that feel like family. And as for the gardens, they won't ever look the same without me, but I know you'll keep them thriving. Middlemoor will always hold a special place in my heart." Danny wiped away a tear, a rare display of emotion for him. He wasn't one to show his feelings so openly, but saying goodbye to Middlemoor and all it represented was almost too much to bear.

They all leaned in for a group hug: Danny, Camilla, Seb, Sally, Karin, and Terry. Even the dogs gathered around them. It was a poignant moment of unity, a testament to the bonds they had forged through shared trials and tribulations.

"I'll drop the keys off on my way out," Danny said as he stepped back.

Danny went out the back door, got into a golf buggy, and drove back to his quarters. The evening concluded in a cascade of tears and heartfelt goodbyes, a solemn reminder of the fractures and farewells that had become all too common in their lives.

The next morning, Camilla descended the stairs to find Danny's keys lying on the doormat, a silent confirmation of his departure. She swallowed the lump in her throat, picked up the keys, and hung them in the cabinet. Determined not to cry, she grabbed her car keys and set off for Plymouth. She had paperwork to sort out, preparations for the work that was soon to begin. Returning to Plymouth without Ben felt surreal and unnerving. Although she often visited various sites alone, this time it was different—it was the last place she'd been before everything fell apart.

As she parked her car and stepped out, she felt a strange sensation of being watched, her ears burning. Across the road, in the offices opposite, an Irishman named David O'Sullivan stood at the window, observing her.

"There's that poor lady, Camilla," David pointed out to his co-worker, Eric.

"Yeah, the wife of that missing man, Benedict Ashworth. Nice man, such a shame."

"She looks sad," David noted, his tone sympathetic.

"Well, I'd think she is given her husband's missing. But I think it's an act. I'm with the media on this one. I think she's involved. Would love to be working on that case but I think they have family lawyers. Typical!" Eric joked as he shovelled in a handful of peanuts.

"What do you mean?" David looked up, puzzled.

"Well, if she is involved and using family lawyers, she'll get away with her husband's disappearance. They'll cover everything up," Eric said, still chewing.

"We shouldn't speculate. Since when do barristers team up with the media anyway?"

"I know, I know. It's just the local gossip. I do think it's suspicious though. She hasn't come from money, she married into the Middlemoor empire, then bam, he's gone missing."

"Wow, no wonder she looks sad. To be going through all that and having everyone blaming her."

"Oh, don't go all soppy. She could be evil for all we know."

"But she could also not be. We shouldn't judge."

"Well, don't go getting involved with all that. You're a young, good-looking chap with a future."

David smiled awkwardly and returned to his desk, but he couldn't stop thinking about Camilla and her ordeal.

Later, as Camilla left the site after a long day, she spotted a man lingering near his car in the car park. It took her a moment to recognise him as someone who attended a recent meeting. He seemed to be hesitating, glancing in her direction as if waiting for her to catch up. She assumed he might have a question about the upcoming construction project. When they were finally side by side, he turned to her with a tentative smile.

"Hi! Uh, sorry to catch you out of the blue, I'm David," he said, lifting a hand in a small wave. "I work just over there."

"Oh, hi, David!" Camilla replied, surprised but smiling. "I remember seeing you a few weeks ago. Is everything okay? Do you have any questions about the work? It'll hopefully be underway soon."

"Aye, I was at the meeting!" He gave a small, awkward laugh and rubbed the back of his neck. "Erm, no, no questions. Actually, I just... I heard about what's going on with Ben, and I... well, I can't imagine how tough that must be."

Camilla smiled as she took in his words. "Thank you, that's kind of you," she said.

David nodded, looking earnest but clearly a bit self-conscious. "I know I'm just a work neighbour," he fumbled slightly, "but I wanted to say if you ever need a break, or just someone to talk to, I'm usually around. No pressure, honestly, just thought I'd mention it."

"That's nice of you. Thanks," she replied, a bit taken aback by his openness but appreciating it all the same.

He hesitated a moment, then handed her his business card with a slightly sheepish smile. "Anytime. And, really, don't feel like you have to reach out if it doesn't feel right. Just know I'm here. Sometimes it's... well, nice to chat with someone you don't know."

Camilla sensed the sincerity in his gesture. "Thanks, I'll keep that in mind."

With a quick, slightly nervous wave, David continued on his way, leaving her with gratitude for his unexpected kindness.

On her drive home, she replayed their conversation in her mind. David had seemed a bit awkward, maybe unsure of how to approach such a sensitive topic. But he clearly meant well, even if he stumbled over his words. She appreciated his compassion. She hadn't expected it, but somehow it had been comforting.

※

Camilla was lying on the sofa in the library, the familiar quiet of the room surrounding her. Suddenly, she heard a faint noise from the hallway that sounded like footsteps. She sat up, calling out, "Seb, is that you? I want you to come see this magazine segment on red carpet fashion." She paused, a smile tugging at her lips as she imagined his sarcastic response. "You'll laugh," she added, waiting for him to appear. But there was nothing. Silence.

A little unnerved, she got up to investigate, calling his name again as she moved towards the hallway. But when she reached it, the space was empty. "Seb?" she called out once more, but no answer came.

Then, a loud bang echoed from the direction of the back kitchen door. Her heart raced as she hurried towards it, hoping it was Ben returning home. When she opened it, there was no one in sight. Stepping outside, she scanned the yard, but all she saw was the garden shrouded in darkness and the eerie stillness of the night.

Confused, she paused for a moment. *It's just the house breathing*, she thought, trying to calm herself. *Probably the wind playing tricks on me. After all, this house is very old.*

Taking a deep breath, she returned to the library. The unsettling feeling still clung to her, but she tried to shake it off as she sank back onto the sofa, telling herself it was nothing. The silence felt thicker now, but she did her best to ignore it.

Chapter Fourteen

Camilla woke up late the next morning, feeling as though she had finally clawed her way back from exhaustion. She had needed the rest, and it was nearing lunchtime by the time she made her way downstairs. The house was eerily quiet—no familiar voices or distant sounds of movement greeted her.

She dropped her hands to her sides and took a deep breath. She paused to compose herself, smoothing her hair and wiping away the remnants of sleep from her eyes. Just then, the kitchen phone rang, its sharp tone slicing through the silence.

Camilla walked down the hallway to the kitchen and picked up the receiver, her heart beating a little faster as she answered.

"Hello?" she said, her voice steady.

"Good morning. Am I speaking with Camilla Stobbs?" The voice on the other end was calm, almost too calm.

"Yes, that's me," Camilla replied, then quickly added,

"well, that was my maiden name. I go by Camilla Ashworth now. May I ask who's calling?"

There was a brief pause, just long enough to deepen the knot forming in Camilla's stomach.

"My name's Victoria," the woman finally said, her tone measured. "I'm from the bereavement support team at West Cornwall Hospital."

Camilla's heart skipped a beat. "Bereavement? I... I'm not sure I understand."

"I'm so sorry to be the one to tell you this, Camilla," Victoria began, her voice softening. "It's about your mother..."

The words hung in the air like a heavy fog that slowly settled over Camilla. For a moment, time itself seemed to stop. The blood drained from her face, and her body went cold.

"No... there must be some mistake," Camilla whispered, her voice barely audible. "I spoke to her yesterday..."

But deep down, she knew. She could feel the truth in the silence that followed.

"I wish there was another way to say this," Victoria continued, her voice full of empathy. "Your mother passed away earlier today. We did everything we could..."

Camilla's hand trembled violently and the phone slipped from her grasp. It swung on its cord, the receiver knocking against the wall as if punctuating the devastating news. The room around her seemed to shift and blur, the colours fading as a high-pitched ringing filled her ears.

This can't be real, she thought, her mind struggling to process the words she had just heard. The walls closed in, the once familiar room now a foreign landscape that offered no comfort.

Through the haze, she could faintly hear Victoria's voice, distant and concerned through the telephone line. "Camilla? Camilla, can you hear me?"

Camilla was struggling to breathe. The walls of the room seemed to close in on her, the air thick with the unbearable pain she felt in her heart. She managed to get to her feet, blind to everything but the overwhelming need to be near something—anything—that reminded her of her mother. Without thinking, she fled the room, her legs carrying her as if by instinct.

She raced up the stairs, her heart pounding so loudly it drowned out all other sounds. The familiar scent of lavender and vanilla lingered in the hallway, guiding her like a beacon to her mother's bedroom. Her hand trembled as she reached for the doorknob, and for a moment she hesitated, terrified of the emptiness that would greet her on the other side. But the need to be close to her mother overpowered her fear, and she pushed the door open.

The room was just as her mother had left it and it was filled with the things she loved. Owl-themed items adorned every corner, each one carefully chosen by Caroline, who had adored the creatures for as long as Camilla could remember. But as her eyes swept across the room, something felt off. The bedcovers were neatly pulled back, the quilt folded at the foot, but the sheets were missing.

The owl-patterned sheets should have been there. Karin had taken them to the dry cleaners and it shouldn't have taken this long to get them back. A shiver ran down Camilla's spine as she walked slowly towards the bed, her mind racing. Why hadn't the sheets been returned?

A sob tore from Camilla's throat as she collapsed onto the bed, burying her face in the pillow that still carried the faintest trace of her mother's perfume. The softness of the quilt beneath her offered no comfort, only a cruel reminder of the person that had been so suddenly and irrevocably taken from her. She reached out blindly, her hands grasping for something to hold on to, something that might anchor her in this storm of sorrow.

Her fingers brushed against her mother's robe, hanging off the edge of the bed. Without thinking, she pulled it close, clutching it to her chest as if it could somehow bring her mother back. The fabric was worn in places from years of use, but it felt like the only solid thing in a world that had just collapsed. As she clung to it, her thoughts kept returning to the missing sheets, the unfinished bed. It gnawed at her, an unsettling reminder that something was not as it should be.

As she buried her face in the robe, her sobs became harder, her body shaking with the force of her anguish. She could almost hear her mother's voice, gentle and soothing, telling her that everything would be alright, that she was there and that Camilla was not alone. But the voice was just a memory, a cruel echo in the emptiness.

And then, through the haze of tears, she felt it—something crinkling against her cheek. She pulled the robe away, her brow furrowing in confusion. There was something inside the pocket, something that felt like paper. Her heart skipped a beat as she reached in, her fingers trembling as they closed around a folded piece of paper.

She pulled it out slowly, her breath catching in her throat as she recognised the handwriting on the front. It was her mother's, elegant and familiar, and it was addressed to her.

To my dearest Camilla

Her vision blurred as fresh tears filled her eyes, and she could barely see the words. Her hands shook as she unfolded the letter; her heart was pounding so hard she thought it might break through her chest.

Taking a deep, ragged breath, she forced herself to focus on the last words her mother had ever written to her.

> Camilla,
>
> I hope you never have to read this letter, but if you are, then my worst fears have come true and I'm no longer with you. I didn't have the heart to tell you in person, especially with Ben missing. It never felt like the right time, and I'm so deeply sorry you had to find out like this.
>
> The truth is, I've been very sick. My breast cancer returned and by the time it was detected, it was at stage 4 and had spread to many areas. I've fought as hard as I could, but there's nothing more the doctors can do. I tried to be strong for you, to keep a brave face during my stay, but every day was a struggle.
>
> Camilla, you are my baby girl, and I love you more than words can express. I am so incredibly proud of you and the strong, compassionate woman you have become. Watching you grow has been the greatest joy of my life.
>
> I hope with all my heart that Ben finds his way back to you. If he hasn't yet, know that I will be his guardian angel, guiding him home to you.

My ashes will be sent to you, and I ask that you spread them around the lake. It's so peaceful there, and always full of owls at night.

Please hold on to our memories, not just as mother and daughter, but as best friends. I will always be with you, in every step you take, in every breath you make.

I'm sorry, my love, for not telling you sooner, and for the pain this letter brings. But know that my love for you is eternal, and I will always be by your side.

Goodnight, my beautiful daughter.
With all my love, Mum xxx

Camilla's hands shook as she finished reading, her tears soaking the paper. The letter slipped from her fingers, fluttering softly to the bed beside her. She clutched her mother's robe even tighter, curling into a ball as waves of grief crashed over her. The reality of her mother's suffering and the immense love behind her words tore through her like a knife, leaving her raw and exposed.

Camilla's tears finally ran dry. She stared at the ceiling above. She couldn't comprehend how everything had fallen apart so rapidly. What had she done to deserve such a cruel fate? She was a kind, caring person, always considerate of others, yet her world was crumbling around her. Desperate for some semblance of comfort, she reached into her pocket, pulled out her phone and David's business card, and sent him a text. She needed to talk to someone—someone who didn't know her intimately, someone who could offer an outside perspective.

> Hello, it's Camilla. I'm so sorry to bother you but I'd like to take you up on that chat if you're free?

Within minutes, David replied.

> Of course! I've just finished some paperwork and was calling it a day anyway. Where would you like to meet?

> Where are you? There is a nice coffee shop in Middlemoor called The Dancing Avocado but not sure if it's far from you?

> Well, I'm actually in Milton Combe, halfway between Plymouth and Middlemoor but if I leave the office now, I can be there in 40 minutes.

> Are you sure? I don't want you to feel like you're driving far. I'm happy to go somewhere else.

> No, honestly, I love trying new coffee shops! It's only 20 minutes from my house anyway.

> OK, perfect. Thank you!

> See you soon!

Walking into the coffee shop, Camilla felt exposed. She was dressed down, her hair messily pulled up, and she wore sunglasses to hide her puffy eyes. She noticed the whispers and stares but tried to ignore them. She saw David sitting in the corner and walked towards him, her heart heavy with grief.

"Hey, thank you for meeting up with me. I know we don't know each other, but I completely agree with what you said about how it's easier to talk to someone you don't know," she said, her voice trembling.

"It's why I gave you my business card. I'm a good listener. It's my job!" David replied gently.

"Oh really, what do you do? I know you work for the law firm across the road, but what do you do there?" she asked.

"I'm a lawyer," David said happily.

"That's impressive. Is it something you've always wanted to do?" Camilla inquired, finding some solace in the small talk.

"Yes, since I was five! I loved watching crime documentaries with my dad and was fascinated by the legal side. It became my ambition," he shared.

"That's amazing. What a passion to have and follow through with! I may actually need your help at some point. You're aware my husband's missing? Everyone thinks I had something to do with it," Camilla said, her voice breaking.

"I did hear, but I'm not making any judgements. I don't understand why people feel the need to voice opinions without knowing the facts. I'm sorry you're going through this," David said sincerely.

"It gets worse," Camilla continued, her voice breaking. "Today, I got a call from the bereavement team at my mother's hospital. She was dying from cancer when she came to visit me but didn't tell me because Ben had gone missing. So now, not only am I dealing with a missing husband and speculation about stealing Middlemoor Estate, but I've also just lost my mother." Tears streamed down her face as she spoke.

David quickly handed her a tissue. "Camilla, I'm so sorry about your mother. I can't begin to imagine what you're going through right now. But... Middlemoor Estate? What's that got to do with Ben's disappearance?" he asked, still trying to process the shock.

"It belonged to the Ashworths for generations. Now, people think I married into the family just to steal it all. I'd give it all up if it meant Ben could come back home," she cried.

"It sounds like a nightmare. I'm happy to help with anything legal-wise," David offered.

"Thank you. I may take you up on that. We have a family legal team, but I'm not sure they're on my side anymore," Camilla admitted.

They continued to sip their coffee, but Camilla's eyes welled up again, and she finally broke down completely.

"Oh, Camilla, come here!" David said, putting his arms around her. "Come on, let's go for some fresh air."

"I best go now. I just feel so sick. Thank you so much for the chat," Camilla said abruptly, leaving the coffee shop.

Chapter Fifteen

It had been a few weeks since Camilla arrived in Penzance to sort out her mother's belongings. Caroline had lived there since Ben bought the house for her after her first breast cancer diagnosis. Caroline didn't need to work as Ben and Camilla insisted on supporting her. In exchange, Caroline helped with data entry for Ward & Ashworth, which she could do from the comfort of her own home. Something Caroline insisted on doing as she didn't want to feel like she sponged off her daughter and son-in-law. Despite their attempts to convince her to move closer to them, Caroline loved her life in Penzance, and they respected her wishes, paying off her mortgage to ease her financial burden.

Camilla finished what she could and stepped out of the house, locking the door behind her. Just then, she heard a familiar voice.

"Hello, Camilla, how are you? It's been a while since I've seen you around. How's your mum? I haven't seen her for a while," Trisha, the neighbour, called out.

"Hi, Trisha," Camilla replied, her voice wobbling slightly. "I'm not doing too well. Mum passed away, so I'm just sorting through her things."

"Oh dear, I'm so sorry. I had no idea!" Trisha said, tears welling up in her eyes.

"It was all a bit of a shock, really. I didn't know she was sick again, but this time it was really bad."

"I had no idea either. The last time I saw her, she looked so well. Oh, pet, come here," Trisha said, walking up to the fence to give Camilla a hug. "Are you holding a local funeral?"

"I think I'm just going to do my own thing. I have her wishes on paper, so I'll honour them. The house will be on the market in the next few weeks. I really hope you get some nice new neighbours."

"No one will ever replace your mother. She was truly amazing. I wish you the best. She'll always be with us," Trisha said, hugging her again.

"Thanks, Trisha," Camilla whispered, feeling the genuineness of her neighbour's kindness.

Carrying a box of papers, Camilla walked to her car. She'd been staying in a hotel for the past few nights, unable to stay in her mother's house alone. It was too hard. Camilla adjusted the satnav, setting the destination for Middlemoor. The journey would take a little over two hours, factoring in the traffic that was beginning to build. As the device calculated the quickest route, she glanced at the fuel gauge and realised she'd need to stop for petrol along the way. Another thought struck her—she was hungry. She hadn't eaten properly for days, and she was determined to avoid the temptation of fast food. Being a Sunday, a comforting roast dinner sounded perfect. With the satnav set and a mental note to find both petrol and a decent meal, she was ready to begin the drive home.

The satnav announced an approaching petrol station, and Camilla signalled to exit the A30. Pulling in, she filled up her car before heading inside to pay. A friendly young man greeted her at the counter.

"Just petrol today?" he asked with a smile.

"Yes, please," Camilla replied. Then, almost as an afterthought, she added, "I don't suppose you know of a good place for a Sunday roast nearby? I'm heading towards Plymouth."

The attendant's face lit up. "Actually, I do! There's a pub about fifteen minutes from here, just off the A30. It's called The Tharp Arms. They do an amazing roast dinner. Ask for Bev or Tom and say Adam sent you. Fantastic couple. They'll sort you out."

Camilla returned his smile. "Thank you!"

Back in the car, she programmed The Tharp Arms into the satnav.

When she arrived, The Tharp Arms exuded the warmth of a traditional English pub. As she stepped inside and found a seat, she noticed the room quieting slightly. Conversations hushed to whispers, and curious glances were cast her way—not because she was dining alone, but because she was Camilla Ashworth, a name now known to everyone after *Tavistock Heritage & Hills'* stories were picked up by other media outlets.

The air buzzed with intrigue, the whispers following her like a shadow. Ignoring the attention, she settled in, determined to enjoy her meal.

This was her life now—under a cloud of suspicion until Ben could be found and her name finally cleared. It struck her how harsh the world could be, how easily people jumped to conclusions. Money seemed to taint everything, projecting shadows even in the brightest of lives. Despite losing her husband and what felt like everything else, all people could think was that she had orchestrated it all for a fortune. The absurdity of it gnawed at her. Why would she need more? She had already married the man she loved and lived a life of luxury. What more could she possibly want? Yet, that was the story they clung to, because in their eyes, wealth changed everything—even the truth.

Finishing up her meal, Camilla felt a wave of contentment wash over her as Bev approached the table.

"How was that for you?" Bev asked.

"Absolutely gorgeous and just what I needed, thank you!" Camilla replied, her voice genuinely appreciative.

"You're welcome, I'm glad you enjoyed it. It's always nice to be recommended, Bev said with a smile. "Can I get you anything else?"

"Just the bill, please. I best get back on the road." Camilla glanced around the room, her discomfort evident as she noticed the lingering stares and whispers that had followed her throughout the meal.

Bev noticed too. Wanting to ease Camilla's discomfort, she offered kindly, "No worries. Let me get Tom to wrap up a piece of cake for you to take home. It's on us."

Camilla's eyes softened, and she managed a small smile, her emotions welling up. "Thank you," she whispered.

Sitting back in the driver's seat of her car, Camilla opened the box Tom had given her. The cake looked too good to resist, so she picked it up and took a bite. The sweet velvety taste melted in her mouth, bringing a momentary sense of peace. Savouring the food, she reached into her bag, pulling out her phone. Before setting off, she decided to text David.

> Hey, I know it's been a few weeks since we talked, but it would be great to see you again when you're free.

She stared out the car window while she continued to enjoy her cake and waited for a reply from David. To her surprise, she received his response much quicker than she had expected.

> Hey, Camilla, I'd love to meet up. I hope you're doing well.

> Perfect! Would you like to come over tomorrow for dinner? I make a really good sausage ragu if Sally lets me in the kitchen, lol!

> Sounds great! I've never had sausage ragu. It sounds nice. Who's Sally, though? Haha.

> Sally's our chef. She's great. You'll get to meet her!

> You have a chef?! That's so cool!!!!

> She is cool! Wait until you meet Sebastian. He's going to like you, haha.

> Oh gosh, how many people am I meeting??

> Erm... a lot. Just the staff. They're all lovely. You'll love them.

The Crimes of Middlemoor Estate

> This sounds bougie. I feel like I need to wear a suit, lmao.

No! Of course not. Just casual. I'll send a taxi to pick you up so you can have a drink!

> Don't be silly. I can order one.

Honestly. Please. What's your address?

> Erm, okay, thank you! It's...

There was a pause. Camilla waited patiently.

> 40 Langford Way, Milton Combe, Plymouth PL6 3FJ.

There was another pause as Camilla booked the taxi.

Taxi booked. It'll pick you up at 6 p.m. It'll be so good to see you. I won't prebook one back in case we play games after dinner, if you fancy it? No pressure. Just want to let my hair down. I'm really good at Monopoly, lol. Terry hates it because I always win! X

> Thank you! I love games. I'm a master at Monopoly. Now, who's Terry? I feel like I need everyone's names so I don't look rude, lol x

Game on then! Terry is the estate's security. He's great. Sounds scary, but he's a soft bear!

> Security?! How big is this place?!

> Big! You'll have to wait and see. It's a beautiful house. See you tomorrow.

> Looking forward to it! Thanks again.

Camilla smiled to herself, but guilt lingered in her thoughts. Should she allow herself to feel excited when her husband was still missing and she had just been sorting through her deceased mother's house? Yes, she decided. She deserved a moment of happiness. The last time she saw David, a few weeks ago over coffee, she had managed to momentarily escape her troubles. It had been a welcome relief. This was why she wanted him to visit again. Although they were still getting to know each other, his presence offered a welcome distraction, and that was needed right now.

She started the car, checked that the satnav was still set for Middlemoor, and proceeded with her route. The drive passed quickly. As she focused on the prospect of David coming for dinner, she found herself able to switch off from her worries, and for the first time in a while, she felt a glimmer of light return.

Chapter Sixteen

The next evening arrived swiftly, and David found himself settling into the back seat of a taxi. As the car wound its way through the picturesque Devon countryside, he couldn't help but admire the lush green fields and rolling hills. It was a huge contrast to the commotion of London and a big part of why David decided to move further down the country.

After about twenty minutes, the taxi approached the grand gates of Middlemoor Estate.

"Wow," David muttered to himself, taken aback by the impressive estate. The gates alone were more luxurious than he had anticipated.

The taxi driver pressed the buzzer.

"Terry speaking. Welcome to Middlemoor Estate. How may I help?" came the voice from the intercom.

"Hello, it's John from Russell's Taxis. I have a guest for you," the driver replied.

"Ah, hello, John! I'll buzz you in now."

The gates slowly opened, and the taxi drove up the long

winding driveway. David could hardly contain his amazement as the mansion came into view, its grandeur accentuated by the soft pink hues of the setting sun. The house, a sprawling masterpiece of architecture, was surrounded by meticulously maintained gardens and vast expanses of land.

Camilla was waiting at the entrance as the taxi pulled up. David stepped out, clutching a bottle of red wine.

"To go with the ragu," he said with a smile, handing her the bottle.

"Oh, thank you, David! You didn't have to bring anything. That's very kind of you. Come in, I'll show you around."

"Thank you. Is the interior of the house as beautiful as the exterior?" he remarked, following her inside.

Camilla led him on a brief tour of the house. It was magnificent, filled with antique furniture, elegant decor, and an air of timeless luxury.

"Do you ever get lost?" David joked, marvelling at the sheer size of the place.

"I did when I first moved in." Camilla laughed.

As they walked down a corridor towards the library, a woman approached them.

"Hello, David. It's very nice to meet you. Sally is just about to serve dinner, so if you both wouldn't mind making your way to the dining room," she said.

"Of course, thank you, Karin," Camilla replied.

"I've poured you both a glass of red," Karin added before heading off.

"That was Karin. She's the housekeeper. Absolutely brilliant at what she does. Everywhere is always so spotless.

Except she misplaced my mother's owl bedspread" Camilla chuckled.

"Owl bedspread?" David asked, intrigued.

"Yes, my mother was obsessed with owls, so I got her a bedspread with owls on it for when she stayed. She loved it! But when Karin took it to the dry cleaners, it got mixed up with someone else's washing and we never saw it again. It's not her fault, but she keeps blaming herself, so I like to pull her leg."

"Oh, I see. Hopefully, it'll turn up when you least expect it," David said.

"Right, are you ready?" Camilla asked, her eyes twinkling with a hint of mischief.

"Ready for what?" David replied, raising an eyebrow.

"Meeting the gang! Watch out for Sebastian. He's going to like you and can be very flirtatious," she said with an awkward smile.

David's eyes widened in mock panic. "I'm a lawyer, don't forget." He winked.

They walked into the dining room, where several people were already seated.

"Everyone, this is David, my friend," Camilla introduced.

"Hello, David, it's nice to meet you." Sally smiled.

"Well, hello, David! My name is Sebastian Julius Archer, but please call me Seb," said a flamboyant man with a dramatic flair, sticking out his tongue playfully followed by a pout. Just the usual for Seb!

"Please, take a seat," Sally said, pulling out a chair.

The table was elegantly set, with plates of delicious food already in place. Casual conversation flowed as everyone got to know David. He quickly became a hit, especially with Seb, who seemed to harbour a hopeful crush.

"So, any updates on Ben?" David asked gently, sensing the undercurrent of sadness among the group.

"Not really," Camilla replied quietly. "It's been a few months now, and there's still no lead. But I'm getting stronger and can talk about it more now."

"Have you thought about a replacement for Danny yet? We'll need to get the gardens back on track," Terry asked between mouthfuls of food.

"Not yet. I know I should start looking, but it's so hard. I feel like Ben should be the one to handle this. I'm only an Ashworth by marriage. It feels like I'd be overstepping," Camilla admitted.

"I've no idea what you mean! You're an Ashworth and you're in charge. You have every right to make decisions about Middlemoor. We're all here to help," Sally reassured her, placing a hand on her arm.

"Thank you." Camilla smiled, her eyes watery.

"Who's Danny and what do you need?" David asked.

"Danny was our gamekeeper and general maintenance man. A man of many talents. He played an important role here at Middlemoor. Not to mention he was handsome and muscly. Actually, a bit like yourself," Seb added, raising his eyebrows, causing everyone to giggle.

"Can I be of help?" David offered.

"As a gamekeeper?" Camilla asked, surprised.

"Yes, I think I could do it. I spent countless weekends planting vegetables, pruning shrubs, and maintaining flower beds with my dad. I'm familiar with the intricacies of soil preparation and the timing of seasonal plantings. Together we installed irrigation systems and designed garden layouts, and Dad took pride in the projects we completed together."

"But what about your lawyer job?"

"I've been thinking about this for a while," he admitted, his tone weary yet sincere. "I came here hoping to get hands-on experience faster than I could in London—it's so competitive there, and I thought a smaller city might be a good stepping stone. But honestly, the work hasn't been as challenging as I'd hoped, and, well... I've ended up falling more in love with the countryside than the career." He gave a small smile. "So, if I can help out until you find someone more permanent, I'd be glad to. Then, I'll head back to London and give the big city another shot. But for now, I'd be happy to stay a little longer, if that works for you. I'm self-employed at my firm so I won't even have to wait out a notice period."

There was another reason he didn't mention: David found Camilla captivating.

"Really? You'd do that for me?" Camilla asked.

"Yes, absolutely."

"Well, I'll match your average monthly income if you can also assist with any legal matters. I'd prefer to avoid the family's legal team if possible, given the circumstances."

"We will?!" Seb exclaimed in surprise.

"Yes, we will," Camilla said firmly, giving Seb a look.

"Oh, I mean, yes, we will," Seb corrected himself, realising the implications.

"Well, the job comes with a fully furnished house if you'd like that too," Camilla added.

David's eyes lit up at the offer. He currently rented a furnished house, so this could work massively in his favour and help him save to buy as that was his aim for the future.

"It's a done deal! And don't worry, Seb, it's not as much as you'd think compared to the average income of a London lawyer!" David joked.

"Great!" Camilla smiled back.

They continued chatting over dinner and through Sally's home-made crème brûlée. Camilla went into more detail about the job and the tasks that needed doing. She felt relieved knowing the back gatehouse wouldn't remain empty for long. The evening was a blend of light-hearted banter and meaningful conversation, a perfect balance that left Camilla feeling hopeful for the first time in a long while.

Several hours of conviviality passed, fuelled by flowing red wine and a lively game of Monopoly, until the evening wore on to 11 p.m. The mood remained cheerful as Sally, Terry, Karin, and Seb decided to call it a night, their laughter still echoing through the halls of Middlemoor.

Camilla and David, however, were not quite ready to end the evening. With their glasses refilled again, they wandered off to the cosy library.

They settled on the sofa directly in front of the crackling fire, the heat from the flames creating a snug, intimate atmosphere. Camilla turned to David, her eyes reflecting the flickering light, and expressed her gratitude once more.

"Honestly, I'm just glad I can help. London will always be there if I want to return. I'm only young. I have time on my side."

Camilla edged closer to David, her proximity

intensifying the connection between them. They shared a lingering look, each silently acknowledging the bond that had formed amidst their individual loneliness. Without another word, they leaned in for a tentative kiss. It was light and tender, a mere brush of lips, yet charged with unspoken emotions.

Pulling back slightly, they gazed into each other's eyes again as the reality of their actions slowly sank in. But the influence of alcohol and the warmth of the moment urged them to take it further. They kissed again, this time with fervent passion. Camilla pushed David into the sofa, their movements causing a delicate vase to tumble off a nearby table and shatter on the floor.

"Oh God, was that expensive?" David asked, his voice laced with concern.

"I've no idea." Camilla giggled, her laughter cutting through the tension as she leaned in for another kiss.

In truth, the vase was extraordinarily valuable. Mrs. Ashworth had purchased it for 1.3 million pounds during an auction in China—a significant loss, though they were oblivious to it in their current state.

They continued their heated embrace, their bodies pressing closer. The wine buzzed through Camilla's veins, blurring the edges of her usual hesitations, making her feel bolder, more uninhibited. David's fingers moved deftly as he unbuttoned her shirt, his touch leaving a tingling feeling that left her breathless. Their breaths quickened as they surrendered to the moment, pulled deeper by a shared longing and the wine's intoxicating haze.

Clothes slipped away, forgotten in the urgency of their connection, and they became utterly lost in each other. But as the haze began to lift, the reality of the night settled over them like a blanket, slowly coaxing them back to their senses.

After a quiet moment, they moved to gather their clothes and pulled each item on with a touch of self-consciousness, as if the cool night air had sobered them both. Camilla ran a hand through her hair, trying to settle the wave of emotions stirred up by the spontaneity of the evening. Her mind was already racing, as guilt mixed with an ache of loneliness and instability.

As she buttoned her shirt, Camilla glanced over at David, her eyes displaying vulnerability. "I'm... I'm sorry. You're probably thinking all sorts about me," she murmured, a hint of regret woven through her words as she wrestled with the effect of the intoxication and her choices.

David shook his head, his expression gentle. "No, no, not at all. Don't think that for a second."

She managed a half smile, her voice uncertain. "It's just... here I am, a woman with a missing husband, my mother recently gone and yet tonight..." Her voice trailed off, and she looked down as if ashamed. "Sometimes, I don't even know what I'm feeling, or what I'm hoping for with everything that's been going on. And tonight, maybe the wine just made everything feel less... complicated. I don't know."

"Camilla," he said softly, reaching for her hand. "You're allowed to feel confused. Tonight wasn't about judgements or expectations. It was just... something I wanted to share with you. You don't need to apologise." He gave her a small smile. "I'm here because I want to be. And I don't want you to think this is something I take lightly. It isn't."

As they straightened up and began to clear away the remnants of the evening, Camilla's mind was already racing, her heart torn between the pleasure of David's presence and the tangle of unresolved feelings she still carried.

"I'd better get a broom to sweep up this vase. I know Seb will notice it's gone, but hopefully he won't make too much of a fuss." Camilla got up to fetch the dustpan and brush. When she returned, David was already on the floor, gathering the larger pieces. They knelt together, cleaning up the shards.

Suddenly, a scratching noise broke the silence. It seemed to be coming from the bookshelf to the left of the fireplace.

"What's that?" David asked, looking puzzled.

"I don't know. I think it's rats. Danny always said it's to be expected in an old house like this. I've never seen anything, so I'm not too worried."

"Well, let this be my introduction to my new job. I'll take a look," David said, moving towards the bookshelf. "Can I touch the books?"

"I guess so," Camilla replied, unaware that special gloves meant for handling the antique books were laid just metres away from them.

David's fingers traced the spines of the books. "Hang on, there's a lever here. Should I pull it?"

"You can give it a go. God knows what it does," Camilla said, joining him.

With a creak, the bookshelf shifted revealing a hidden passage behind it. The air was musty and stale; the darkness almost seemed endless, stretching infinitely with no sign of light or relief in sight.

"What on earth?"

"I guess by your reaction that you didn't know about this secret passageway?" David asked.

"No! I mean, the house is bound to have secret

passageways that scullery maids might have used back in the day, but no one's mentioned any that have been found."

They cautiously entered the passage, their phone flashlights piercing the gloom. The corridor stretched behind the fireplace, leading them deeper into the unknown.

"This is creepy. I feel like I'm in one of those YouTube videos exploring abandoned places," Camilla said, her laugh shaded with nervousness.

"It's definitely creepy and dusty. It doesn't look like it's been used in years."

The passage smelled old—not damp, but ancient and untouched. As they turned a corner, they reached a dead end, where an old wooden sideboard stood against the wall. Beneath it was a barely visible trapdoor.

"What do you think it is?" Camilla asked, her curiosity piqued.

"Hmm, my guess would be a possible priest hole, but I could be wrong. We could look?" David suggested.

"Yes! We must look! I'm intrigued. Maybe it leads deeper into the house? I have the blueprints somewhere, and this is definitely not on them."

"Could be one of those stories where someone's secretly living inside the walls!" David said with a grin.

"Oh God, don't even joke about that!" Camilla responded, half horrified, half laughing.

David moved the table aside and lifted the stiff trapdoor, revealing a rope tie and a small hook to hold it open securely. They peered down to see a tall narrow room with a small ladder against one wall.

"You want to go in?" David asked.

"Absolutely! We might find treasure!"

David descended first then helped Camilla down the

ladder. Their flashlights revealed a small enclosed space: an old abandoned priest hole, but it was not as empty as they expected.

Two skeletons lay within the dimly lit room. One was propped awkwardly against the back wall, its bones draped in the tattered remnants of a once-white female's nightgown. The other skeleton, sprawled on the cold hard floor, wore what remained of a man's nightshirt, and had a rope tightly knotted around its neck. The rope was connected to a hook in the ceiling, suggesting a grim and tragic end. In the far corner, two dusty suitcases, covered in a thick layer of cobwebs, seemed to watch over the scene, their worn leather and rusty clasps whispering secrets of long-forgotten lives.

"What. The. Fuck!" Camilla gasped, turning to bury her face in David's shoulder.

"We need to call the police immediately!" David said, his voice trembling with urgency. They scrambled out of the room, their hearts pounding violently from the horrifying discovery.

Back in the library, Camilla fumbled to call 999, her hands shaking uncontrollably. The chilling and ghastly revelations of the hidden room had transformed their evening into a nightmarish ordeal, one far darker and more sinister than anything they could ever have imagined.

Chapter Seventeen

It was almost 1 a.m. and the grounds of Middlemoor Estate were swarming with police. Camilla was wrapped in a blanket, shivering not from the cold but from the night's revelations. David and the staff stood beside her; their pale faces said it all. The front of the grand house, once a symbol of peace and stability, now felt like the epicentre of a nightmare, again.

DS Ransome approached, his expression grave.

"Hi, everyone. First, I want to thank Camilla and David for their statements. Camilla, I'm sorry to confirm this, but it seems you've uncovered your missing in-laws this evening. We found a murder-suicide note beside Mr. Ashworth, and it's clear to us what has happened. We're closing the case now, and after an autopsy on both remains, we'll be able to release the bodies if you wish to proceed with funeral arrangements."

Camilla's stomach churned. "I had a feeling it was them. But why?"

The officer nodded sympathetically. "I've scanned Mr.

Ashworth's note as I thought you should have a copy, especially if Ben returns home. We've had to keep the original, of course, but as of now, the case will be closed. I'm so sorry you had to find this."

The staff stood in disbelief. Two people they cared so much for had been in the house this whole time, and no one had suspected a thing. It was a lot to digest. Camilla's hands trembled as she unfolded the letter.

> I deeply regret that you had to discover what you've found. I took these actions because my love for my wife is so profound that the thought of life without her was unbearable. I uncovered her affair with Danny, our gamekeeper, and though I do not know when it began or how long it might have continued before I found out, I couldn't face the possibility of losing her. Rather than confront her, I waited for the moment we were to depart on a trip and put my plan into motion.
>
> On the night we were to leave, I suffocated her with a pillow while she slept, ensuring she would never leave me. I then moved our packed suitcases into the secret room, sealing it behind us. I left the light on, though I imagine the bulb will have burned out long before we are found. Afterwards, I tied a rope around my neck, fastened it to a hook in the ceiling and

kicked the chair away, so that we could be together in death as we were in life.

You won't find our phones; I disposed of them in the lake. If we are discovered in recent years, please let Benedict know that he was loved deeply by us both, and that I hope he has led a happy, healthy life filled with children of his own.

This was not an easy decision, but now, at last, we are together forever.

Signed,
Henry Magnus Ashworth

Wow, thought Camilla. Someone would eventually have to call Danny and explain what had happened, but not now. Not tonight.

"Terry, would you please mind taking David home?" she asked.

"No, no, I'll call a taxi," David protested.

"Honestly, it's fine, David, I don't mind," Terry insisted.

"Only if you're sure?"

"Absolutely, I'm positive."

"Thank you for this evening. I'm sorry it ended up like this," David said, turning to Camilla.

"I should be thanking you. Although it was a grisly find, you've helped solve the case of my missing in-laws, and I'll be forever thankful for that."

Camilla gave David a hug goodbye, and everyone went their separate ways. The night had stretched into the early hours of the morning, and it was clear it was time for everyone to get some much-needed rest given the night's events.

Camilla managed to get at least six hours of sleep, but the rest was fitful. Knowing forensics were still about and police cordoning off the grounds made her uneasy. She made her way downstairs with sleepy eyes.

"Good morning, Camilla. How are you feeling?" Seb asked, putting his arms out. As Camilla reached out to hug him, her tears told all.

Suddenly, there was a knock at the door. It was a special delivery. Caroline's ashes. Not really what Camilla needed at that moment, but they were always going to arrive at some point. She grabbed the keys to the golf buggy and made her way through the woods towards the lake, just as her mother had requested. The sun was shining: a cruel contrast to her inner feelings. Camilla walked over to the lake and stood by the water's edge. She began to say a few words.

"Mum, I'm so heartbroken. My chest feels empty without you. I wish you'd told me what you were going through—I would have never let you go that day. I would have stayed by your side until your very last breath. All I want is to hold you one more time, to feel your embrace and inhale the scent of your perfume. Those little things that won't be possible anymore."

At that moment, an owl appeared from nowhere and settled on the wooden post of the platform to the water. In broad daylight. A tear rolled down Camilla's smiling cheeks. She knew this owl was her mother.

"I love you, Mum. You'll always be my best friend."

Camilla scattered her mother's ashes into the water. Each tear felt like a final goodbye. She poured the last of the ashes and smiled at the owl just before it decided to fly away. Getting back into the golf buggy, she wiped her face and made her way back to the house. Thankfully, forensics and the police were finishing up.

"Hello, Mrs. Ashworth, we're all done now," Ransome said, taking his hat off and placing it on his chest. "Are you okay?"

"I'll have to be. It will just take time, I think," she replied, smiling with watery eyes.

"You've been through a lot, and it's all happened so quickly. Please don't hesitate to reach out if you need help. I have some amazing contacts in all areas of therapy."

"Thank you, Detective Sergeant Ransome. I really appreciate that and all you and your team's efforts. I'm just hoping for a safe return from Benedict."

"We'll keep trying," he assured her before walking off to his car.

Everyone had left. Not even the staff were around. Camilla went up to her room to make herself look a little bit more presentable. She'd been texting David most of the morning, keeping him posted on the forensics. He was aware her mother's ashes had arrived, so he knew it had been a horrific day so far. He'd asked if she'd like to meet for coffee in Plymouth. Get away from Middlemoor for a bit. Camilla got there safely, but she didn't remember the actual driving. She was so zoned out that the forty-minute drive felt like forty seconds. She parked her car on a side street and made her way to Ruben's Café Noir, a coffee shop David often visited as it was close to his office. As she walked around the corner, the coffee shop came into sight, but as she got closer more people gathered on the path. She realised it was the media. They began snapping pictures of her and getting in her way. She tried to shield herself, and tears began running down her face.

"Where's Ben?" one shouted.

"How did you find Mr. and Mrs. Ashworth? Did you know they were inside the house this whole time?" another piped up. They continued to shout questions about something they had no idea about.

"Are you trying to steal the estate?"

"Is this an inside job?"

"Leave me alone!" Camilla yelled.

David came rushing out when he saw all the commotion from inside. "Camilla, quick! Get away from her!" He pushed past them all and guided Camilla into the coffee shop. People were staring. It was huge news across Devon and the UK. Her life felt like a movie but not a good one. One that was never-ending. How did the media know she was heading to Ruben's Café Noir? And of course, she happened to be meeting a man which was sure to fuel the rumours!

"I just can't do it. I can't be here right now. I'm trying to stay afloat, run a business, search for my missing husband, grieve my mother's death, and try to erase the image of my dead in-laws. How? How am I meant to carry on?"

"I wish there was something I could say that would be helpful," David said, reaching for her arm.

BANG, BANG, BANG.

Camilla turned around to see more media gathered outside, pressing against the windows and flashing their cameras, as if they were wielding pitchforks.

"Hi, guys, I've called the police to come deal with the mob outside. Let me get you some coffees." The kind barista spoke softly.

"You know what, could we please get two lattes to go? I need to get her away from here," David said.

"Yes, absolutely, let me get them done quickly. It's on the house!"

Within minutes, she returned with two lattes and a small bag of cakes. "Come this way, out the back. Don't wade through them lot."

"Thank you." Ben grabbed Camilla's bag, the coffees, and cakes, then took her by the arm.

As they left through the rear exit, the sound of police sirens filled the air. They rushed to David's car that was parked down a nearby street.

"I'm going to take you on a walk, somewhere quiet and secluded where we can talk, and you can scream and let everything out," David said softly.

Camilla nodded, wiping her tears and nose with a tissue. David drove towards a small public bridleway just outside of Plymouth. They drove in silence, except for Camilla's occasional sniffle. As they approached the lay-by, her breathing became erratic, each breath more laboured than the last. By the time David pulled up, Camilla was hyperventilating. Her cries turned into deep wrenching sobs as she clutched her chest. "It hurts so much, David," she gasped. "I just need my mum."

David jumped out and rushed to the passenger side. He opened the door and gently helped her out, but her legs gave way. She collapsed to the ground, and David went down with her, wrapping his arms tightly around her. He held her close as she wept uncontrollably, her pain pouring out in waves.

"It's okay, Camilla. Let it all out. I'm here for you," he murmured, rocking her gently. The world around them faded away as they sat on the gravel, Camilla's tears soaking David's shirt. His presence, solid and unwavering, was the anchor she desperately needed in that moment of overwhelming grief. Minutes stretched into what felt like hours as Camilla's sobs gradually subsided. Her body was exhausted from the emotional storm. David continued to hold her, his steady breathing a calming rhythm against her. Eventually, she pulled back slightly and looked up at him with red-rimmed eyes.

"Thank you, David," she whispered, her voice hoarse.

He brushed a strand of hair from her face and gave her a reassuring smile. "We'll get through this together," he said.

With a gentle hand, he helped her to her feet, and they got back in the car. Believing it wasn't safe for her to drive home, he took her back and planned to arrange for Terry to bring her car home.

In the garden at Middlemoor, Sally and Seb were chatting. Sebastian was lying on a lounger with a cocktail in his hand, while Sally stood nearby, looking out into the garden.

"Seb, the sun's out, but it's hardly warm. Why are you lounging like you're sunbathing?" Sally asked, amusement in her voice.

"Well, it's been such a week, I need to at least pretend I'm on holiday. Plus, I'm trying to think of the right words to use when I call Danny," Seb replied, swirling the cocktail in his glass.

"What do you mean?"

"Someone's going to have to tell him at some point. If the letter is true, then he needs to know his secret lover is deceased. He needs to mourn too."

"Yes, I suppose you're right. I can't help you there, I'm afraid. I can't even find the words myself. I still feel like it's a nightmare I'm going to wake up from eventually."

"Agreed. I miss them. I miss Mr. Ashworth walking around, making dry jokes that I often believed, and Mrs. Ashworth constantly scolding him for being a miserable git," Seb said, removing the cocktail stick and eating one of the olives from his dirty Martini.

"Me too. I miss Mr. Ashworth rubbing his hands together every time I presented his food, and Mrs. Ashworth chasing after him with a napkin to wipe the food off his chin that he would say he was saving for later," Sally reminisced, a sad smile on her lips.

The Crimes of Middlemoor Estate

They both stared out into the garden, lost in their memories.

"I think David is moving into Danny's old place this afternoon," Sally said, breaking the silence.

"Yes, I think you're right. I should know, as the estate manager, but my head is so scrambled these days that I have no idea what's going on anymore," Seb replied, taking a swig of his drink.

"My role certainly hasn't changed. Everyone is still chowing down the food I make, but I guess you could say I have fewer servings to plate up these days." Sally sighed deeply. "Right, I'd best crack on with my veg. The slow-roasted pork is already cooking nicely."

"Argh, Sally, I do love a bit of porking," Seb said with a cheeky grin and his signature wink.

"Oh gosh, on that note, see you later!" Sally chuckled as she walked away, shaking her head.

Tavistock Heritage & Hills

Mystery of Ashworths' Disappearance Solved After Grim Discovery at Middlemoor House of Horrors

A chilling turn of events unfolded last night at Middlemoor Estate when Camilla Ashworth and a mystery man, who we can now reveal is David O'Sullivan, uncovered the remains of Mr. and Mrs. Ashworth in a hidden room of the property. The discovery has come after years of uncertainty surrounding the couple's disappearance, which had baffled both the community and authorities.

Around 1 a.m., police arrived to investigate the grisly scene. The bodies, long presumed missing, were identified through a murder-suicide note left beside Mr. Ashworth, confirming the tragic sequence of events.

The letter, penned by Henry Ashworth himself, detailed the harrowing actions that led to their deaths. Ashworth, devastated by the discovery of his wife's affair with the gamekeeper, Danny, took matters into his own hands. The note outlined how he suffocated his wife before ending his own life, choosing to be together in death rather than live without her.

DS Ransome confirmed the findings, stating that the case will be officially closed after autopsies are conducted on the remains. "We'll proceed with funeral arrangements once everything is finalised," he said.

For Camilla, the discovery will have been both a relief and a horror as her in-laws had been in the house the whole time. There is still no sign of her missing husband. The investigation has concluded, but the tragedy of the Ashworths' fate will haunt Middlemoor Estate forever.

But one question lingers: What is the relationship between David O'Sullivan and Camilla? Was he merely a source of comfort, or does his presence tie into the growing whispers that Camilla herself might be the reason her husband disappeared? As the last Ashworth remains missing, we ask, has history repeated itself?

Chapter Eighteen

After dropping Camilla off, David headed back to his office in Plymouth. Although today should have been his last day, he had taken annual leave but still needed to collect the final items from his desk and return his keys to his manager.

He hadn't left much time to do so, as he was supposed to be back at Middlemoor by 5 p.m. to meet Sebastian for an induction to his new role as gamekeeper. He knew there was a possibility he'd be late, which wouldn't look good on his first day, but it had been important to make sure Camilla got home safely after the day's earlier events. It had been heartbreaking to watch. Seb would understand, so David sent him a quick text.

David entered the building and walked towards the lift, feeling eyes on him. When he went into the office, everyone turned to look at him. The tension in the air was palpable. The silence was only broken by a cough from Fred who was sitting in the corner.

Gerald, his boss, approached him.

"You alright, David?" Gerald asked.

"Yes, thank you. Just here to grab my last bits," David replied, reaching into his pocket and pulling out his keys. "And give these back." He handed them to Gerald.

"Are you sure you want to go? You're so good at what you do, and you've got such a career ahead of you. I believe you could be the best in your generation!" Gerald tried to push the keys back.

"Yes, I'm sure," David said.

"It's just, you know..." Gerald trailed off, glancing around the room.

The silence grew thicker; everyone was listening intently.

"No, Gerald, I don't know!" David replied, his frustration evident.

"House of horrors. We all saw the newspaper this morning... and your name's in it," Gerald whispered, leaning in closer.

David turned to face everyone. "I know what you're all thinking, and no, I'm not crazy for leaving a perfectly stable job to do something I've never really done before!! Well, when you put it like that, it does sound kinda crazy, but honestly, whatever rumours you've heard, you have it all wrong," he said firmly. He turned back to his desk, grabbed the pile of his stuff, and faced his colleagues one final time. "Thank you all for everything, and good luck with your futures."

As he turned to leave, he heard Annalee, the office gossip, mutter under her breath, "You'll need the luck!" She smirked as she spoke. David took a deep breath, closed his eyes momentarily to compose himself, and then walked out without looking back. He had no intention of responding to what she said. He had made his choice and was resolute in sticking to it.

As the sun dipped in the sky, signalling the approach of dinnertime, Sally continued her preparations in the kitchen. Karin set an extra place at the table, which would now be a permanent addition for David. Just then, David's car pulled up to the front of the house.

"Oooh, that's David!" Seb exclaimed, peering through the kitchen window before rushing to the front door.

"Well, hello, Mr. O'Sullivan! Let me take you to your new humble abode," Seb greeted him kindly.

"Hello, Seb, yes please do! I'm super excited to be joining you guys now," David replied with a smile.

"Oh, is this all you have? Just two suitcases?"

"Yes, I don't own much. I was renting a furnished place, so these are my personal belongings."

"Perfect. You're at the back of the estate, so we can either drive around in your car or take the golf buggy."

"Erm, I think the golf buggy would be fun, and then I can drive back after dinner. Maybe take my car via the main road afterwards?"

"No, darling, we'll be having a full-bodied white wine with dinner, so let's drive your car now and I can get Karin to meet us with a buggy."

"That sounds like a better plan," David agreed.

Seb hopped into David's car, and directed him on to the main road. They followed the winding brick wall that bordered the extensive grounds to David's new cottage at the rear entrance of Middlemoor Estate. It was a cosy little place, nestled among the trees, with a charming view of the rolling hills.

They dropped off his bags and Seb gave David a brief tour, pointing out a few security features to ensure he felt comfortable. Karin arrived and they hopped onto the golf buggy and went back.

As they approached the house, the smell of dinner wafted through the air. Sally had outdone herself with a sumptuous feast, and Karin had set the table beautifully. David soaked up the warm welcome as he joined the others for the meal.

The conversation flowed easily over dinner, with laughter and stories filling the room. The wine complemented the delicious pork dish perfectly, and the evening stretched on in a lively atmosphere.

By the time they finished, the moon had risen high in the sky. David felt a deep sense of belonging, knowing he had found not just a place to work but a new home. As the night grew late, the group dispersed, leaving David to reflect on his first night with his new family. He then made his way back to his cottage on the golf buggy. The cool night air brushed against his face as the estate's lights twinkled softly in the distance. The path was serene, lined with ancient trees whose leaves whispered secrets on the breeze.

As he approached his new home, nestled cosily among the greenery, he couldn't help but feel he'd made the best decision ever.

He parked the buggy and took a moment to admire the quaint structure, its silhouette bathed in the gentle glow of the moonlight.

The Crimes of Middlemoor Estate

David stepped inside; the interior still carried the fresh scent of recent preparations. He moved through the rooms, each one a blend of rustic charm and modern comfort. The soft lighting created an inviting feeling. He unpacked a few personal items and placed them carefully around to make the space feel more like home.

Finally, David made his way to the bedroom. The bed, with its crisp linens and fluffy pillows, had that hotel feel. He changed into his nightwear, and the day's excitement and exhaustion settled over him. As he lay down, the mattress seemed to embrace him and he pulled the blanket up to his chin. The quiet of the night was punctuated only by the distant sounds of nature.

David's thoughts drifted to the day's events and the generous welcome he'd received. It felt like the beginning of a new chapter. The room, the estate, and the people had all contributed to a deep sense of contentment.

As he closed his eyes, the fatigue from the day's activities quickly took over. His breathing slowed and he surrendered to sleep, comforted by the thought that he was exactly where he was meant to be. David slept soundly, ready to embrace the new opportunities and experiences that awaited him at Middlemoor Estate.

Chapter Nineteen

Over time, David truly settled in. The newspapers, which had once fixated on Middlemoor Estate, had long since moved on, leaving the residents of the estate to settle into a quiet rhythm.

Each day brought new experiences and skills, from mastering the art of grass cutting to perfecting intricate hedge trimming patterns. His bond with the staff grew stronger, and he'd never felt more at home. His relationship with Camilla deepened as well, and it was clear that his feelings were reciprocated. It had been almost a year since Ben had gone missing, and while he was not forgotten, Camilla knew she couldn't put her life on hold forever.

One bright morning, Sally and Karin were outside having their morning coffee, enjoying the tranquil view of the gardens. Gardens that David had been diligently tending to with great effort.

As they were discussing their plans for the day, David approached with a contemplative look.

"I've been considering a trip to the South of France for

Camilla," he proposed. "It would be a wonderful, relaxing break for her."

Sally seemed hesitant at first, her protective nature evident. But with Karin's gentle reminder about the importance of moving forward, she began to see the merit in David's idea.

"Time has passed, Sally," Karin said softly. "A change of scenery might be just what she needs."

Seb, overhearing the conversation, couldn't help but join in enthusiastically.

"I think it's a splendid idea!" he exclaimed. "I can check her diary. And maybe I could come along in case you need anything while you're away?"

David chuckled. "I was thinking just the two of us, Seb."

Seb blushed slightly. "Oh yes, of course, duh!"

Pulling out the ever-present diary, Seb flipped through the pages. "I can't see anything scheduled from Sunday through to Wednesday. Why don't you book it for tomorrow and make it three nights?"

Karin smiled. "Well, it'll certainly be a surprise."

"Do it! She'll love the break," Sally agreed. "I can't remember the last time she went away for something other than dealing with her mother's affairs."

David's face lit up with excitement. "Let's get it booked, then. I'm not good at keeping surprises but I can keep it until tomorrow. It'll be perfect! I'd better go finish cutting the last bit of lawn so everything is taken care of for a few days!" He beamed and hurried off, his enthusiasm contagious.

As David wrapped up his tasks for the day, his thoughts kept drifting to the surprise he had planned for Camilla. He could already picture the joy on her face when she found out. With a sense of excitement, he made the booking, ensuring everything was just right. That evening, he finally shared the news with Camilla. Her eyes widened with surprise, quickly followed by a smile of pure delight.

Early the next morning, they set off for the airport. The car ride was filled with easy laughter and a growing sense of anticipation as the stress and strain of the past year slowly began to fade. With each passing mile, they felt a little lighter, a little closer to the peace they both craved. When they touched down in France, the sight of the picturesque countryside offered a tranquil escape from the demands of their everyday lives.

As they settled into the rhythm of their first day exploring a charming village and sampling exquisite wines, they relished simply being together and Camilla visibly relaxed. The serene landscapes, the gentle heat of the sun, and the quiet moments shared between them brought a sense of calm and renewal, as if the troubles of the past were being washed away and replaced by a renewed sense of hope and connection.

The Crimes of Middlemoor Estate

Keith put down the phone, took a deep breath, and let the load of the conversation settle in his mind. He slumped back in the chair of Middlemoor's home office, exhaustion etched on his face. He never thought he'd find himself working on a Sunday morning.

Sally walked in with a much-needed cup of tea and a generous slice of home-made carrot cake.

"What's up?" she asked, noticing his troubled expression.

Keith sighed. "It's another local project pulling out."

"Is that even allowed?" she inquired, incredulous.

"Yes, unfortunately. They haven't signed anything yet," he replied. "With everything that's happened over the past year, people don't want to work with Ward & Ashworth."

"Could this turn into a financial issue?" Sally probed, her worry growing.

"Absolutely not," Keith assured her, though his confidence wavered slightly. "I don't want to fail Henry or Warden but I have to admit my morale's dropping, and I want to be working on bigger things."

Sally nodded, understanding his frustration. "I know how much this means to you. You've put in so much work."

"It's disheartening," Keith continued, taking a sip of the tea. "I feel like we're stuck, and every setback makes it harder to stay motivated. I want to achieve more, to contribute something significant."

Sally placed a reassuring hand on his shoulder. "You're doing everything you can. Sometimes things don't go as planned, but that doesn't mean you're failing. It's tough at the moment, but you have to stay strong."

Keith nodded, grateful for her support. "You're right. It's just hard to see the light at the end of the tunnel right now.

But I need to keep pushing forward, for Henry and for the team. We'll find a way through this."

Sally smiled. "Exactly. And remember, you're not alone in this. We're all in it together."

Keith took another deep breath, feeling a bit more resolute. "Thanks, Sally. I needed that."

"Anytime," she replied, handing him the slice of carrot cake. "Now, eat this and let's figure out our next steps. We'll tackle this one day at a time."

Chapter Twenty

For most, it was a bright and sunny Tuesday morning. Despite it being the school holidays, Plymouth beach wasn't busy yet, but a few people were already enjoying themselves. It was the perfect setting for one family in particular—the Taylors. They had set up their spot, nice and early, complete with an umbrella, chairs, blankets, and a cool box full of refreshments. The sand was inviting, and the sea sparkled under the sun.

Mr. and Mrs. Taylor were lounging on their deckchairs, enjoying a rare moment of relaxation, while their two children, ten-year-old Katie and younger brother Charlie, were building an elaborate sandcastle nearby. Laughter and the sound of playful chatter filled the air.

Katie's attention drifted towards the water. Something floating near the shore caught her eye. Intrigued, she stood up and brushed the sand off her shorts.

"Look, Charlie! I found treasure!" she shouted, but Charlie was too engrossed in his sandcastle to pay any attention.

Katie's curiosity got the better of her, and she wandered off closer to the water's edge. The object bobbed gently on the waves, just within reaching distance. She waded into the shallow surf; the cool water was a contrast to the warm sand. As she reached for the floating ball, something unseen wrapped around her ankle, pulling her off balance.

She fell into the water, her head momentarily submerged as she fought to stay afloat. Panic set in as she couldn't set her foot free. Her cries for help were muffled by the sounds of the waves, but her father, glancing up from his book, saw her waving arms and immediately knew something was wrong.

"Katie!" Mr. Taylor shouted, leaping up and sprinting towards the water. Mrs. Taylor, hearing the urgency in his voice, followed closely behind. The seconds felt like hours as he reached for his daughter and lifted her to safety. Katie was coughing and crying, clinging to her father as he placed her down on one of their chairs.

"What on earth were you doing? I've told you loads of times about the dangers of water, especially the sea!" Mrs. Taylor's voice was shaking.

"It's her foot," Mr. Taylor said, noticing the plastic bag twisted around her ankle.

Mrs. Taylor knelt down and began to untangle it. She pulled it free; her face went pale. Inside the bag was a gruesome sight—a human head, its features distorted but unmistakable. She dropped the bag in horror and screamed, catching the attention of nearby beachgoers.

Pandemonium engulfed the beach as people realised what was happening. Mr. Taylor called the local police while Mrs. Taylor held both Katie and Charlie, shielding them from the sight. The police arrived quickly, cordoned off the area and began taking statements. Katie, still shaken, clung to her mother, her earlier excitement about finding "treasure" replaced with horror. The idyllic day at the beach had turned into a nightmare, one that would haunt the Taylor family for a long time to come.

At Middlemoor Estate, Sally glanced at the kitchen clock as she grabbed her shopping list from the counter. It was already midday and she still had so much to do. Leaving the cosy confines of home, she stepped into the summer sun, the list clutched tightly in her hand.

As she navigated the familiar roads of the village, her thoughts drifted to various errands she had to complete. The food shop was first on the list, followed by a quick stop at the pharmacy.

She had just turned on to the main road when her phone rang. Glancing at the screen, she saw it was Camilla. Smiling, she answered the call through her car's Bluetooth system.

"Hey, Camilla!"

"Hi, Sally! Just checking in. Any updates?" Camilla's voice was cheerful and she sounded relaxed.

"Nothing new here. How's the South of France treating you?"

"Oh, it's wonderful! We've been keeping our phones off as much as possible, just trying to chill out and live in the moment. David and I have been exploring the local villages, enjoying the food, and just soaking up the sun."

"That sounds perfect. You definitely deserve the break,"

Sally said, imagining the picturesque scenes Camilla must be experiencing.

"It really is. I didn't realise how much I needed this until we got here. The weather's been fantastic, and the people are so friendly. It's been a dream."

"I'm so glad to hear that. Enjoy every minute of it," Sally said sincerely. "I'll see you tomorrow evening when you get back."

"Absolutely. We'll catch up then. Take care, Sally."

"You too, Camilla. Enjoy the rest of your holiday!"

The call ended, and Sally felt pleased for Camilla. She focused back on the road, a content smile on her face, thinking about the reunion tomorrow. With Camilla's happiness lingering in her thoughts, she continued on her way, ready to tackle the rest of the day.

Sally pulled her car into a parking space at Tesco and turned off the engine. She grabbed her reusable shopping bags from the passenger's seat and exited the car. She made straight for the row of trolleys and selected one with a smooth roll.

With her shopping list in hand, Sally wandered up and down the familiar aisles of the store, her mind on the mundane task of replenishing the fridge for Camilla and David's return. As she turned into the dairy aisle and reached for a carton of milk she overheard a phone conversation from a nearby shopper.

"Did you hear? They found a human head on Plymouth beach this morning," the woman whispered urgently into her phone.

Sally froze, her hand hovering over the milk. Her heart began to race as snippets of the conversation replayed in her head. She slowly pulled back from the milk and stood still for a moment, absorbing the shock.

Without completing her shopping, Sally wheeled the trolley to the rack and hurried back to her car. She fumbled for her phone and rang DS Ransome, but there was no answer. Frustration and anxiety built up as she sped towards the beachfront.

Upon arrival, she saw the police presence was overwhelming. Blue tape cordoned off a significant portion of the beach. Sally parked her car hastily and approached the scene, slipping under the tape in desperation to get closer.

"Sorry, you can't be here!" a police officer said, stopping her.

"Please, let me through!" she pleaded, catching the attention of Ransome nearby. Recognising her, he signalled for the officer to let her through.

"Sally, what are you doing here?" Ransome asked, concerned.

"Is it Ben?" Sally blurted out, her voice trembling.

The detective sighed, glancing towards the scene. "We can't tell yet. The head is too water-damaged to identify immediately. We'll need dental records."

Sally felt a surge of helplessness and panic. Without waiting for more information, she turned and ran, her mind a whirlwind of fear and uncertainty.

Back in her car, she gripped the steering wheel, her knuckles white. She needed answers, but all she had were more questions. The drive to Middlemoor was a blur as the news of the discovery hung over her like a dark cloud, but she needed to get her errands done too.

Sebastian stood on the front porch, his phone pressed against his ear. He glanced at his watch for the sixth time, his stomach twisting. Sally still wasn't picking up. The news about the head washing up on the shore had spread like wildfire and it had shaken him to his core. He needed to see Sally to make sure she was okay.

Letting out a tense sigh, he ended the call and shoved his phone in his pocket, eyes fixed on the empty driveway as shadows crept across the sprawling lawns. Just as he was thinking about trying to ring her again, her red car came into view, winding up the drive. Relief washed over him, though it didn't fully ease his worry.

When she parked and stepped out of the vehicle, he could see the strained look on her face, even from a distance. Neither of them said a word as she closed the car door. She broke into a run, and he moved towards her, meeting her halfway. They embraced tightly, the weight of the day's fears shared wordlessly between them. Sebastian buried his face in her hair, feeling her shake slightly in his arms, the dampness of her tears pressing against his cheek.

After a moment, Sally pulled back just enough to look up at him, her eyes wide, searching. "You heard, didn't you?"

He nodded, his hands still on her shoulders, steadying her. "Yeah... I heard," he murmured.

She swallowed. "Who could do something like that? That poor little girl... she'll never forget this day. It... it feels like a nightmare."

He took a deep breath and pulled her close again, hoping his presence could offer some comfort. "I don't know, but whatever happens, we'll face it together."

As everyone sat down for dinner, the tantalising aroma of takeout Chinese food filled the air. Sally, feeling a bit self-conscious about not cooking, said, "I'm sorry I didn't make anything tonight."

Terry dismissed her apology with a smile. "Don't be daft, Sally. This is perfect. We don't get takeaway often, so it's a nice treat—and you deserve a break."

Sebastian, always keen on adding a touch of ceremony, suggested an invocation. "How about we say a prayer before we start?"

Everyone else exchanged hesitant glances, feeling a bit out of their element. "Erm..." they mumbled collectively, unsure how to respond. But Sebastian was insistent, raising his hands slightly as if to summon divine inspiration.

He began his prayer with a flourish. "Dear, Lord, we thank you for this bountiful feast we are about to receive. Bless the hands that prepared it, and may it nourish our bodies and souls." His voice took on a dramatic tone, and his eyes closed tightly, as if he were channelling some deep spiritual connection.

Terry shifted uncomfortably in his seat, his awkwardness obvious and a bit humorous. He glanced at the others, who tried to stifle their giggles at Sebastian's theatrics.

After what felt like an eternity, Sebastian finally

concluded his prayer with a hearty "Amen and we hope that the head found isn't Ben's". Everyone echoed the amen, with mixed emotions about the ending but eager to dig into the food.

They began to eat, the tapping of chopsticks and the hum of contented munching filling the room. As they savoured the variety of dishes, Sally broached a sensitive topic. "I think we should avoid mentioning anything to Camilla until she gets back. There's no point in worrying her. She needs to enjoy her last night away."

The others nodded in agreement. "Absolutely," Terry said between bites of sweet and sour chicken. "She deserves a break. No need to burden her with any problems right now."

"Agreed," Sebastian said, his earlier dramatics giving way to genuine concern. "But won't she have seen it on social media? It's everywhere."

"I don't think so," Sally replied. "She mentioned earlier that she's had her phone off most of the time. I'm sure she would have called if she knew."

The conversation then shifted to lighter topics, with stories and laughter filling the room. They talked about their favourite Chinese dishes, reminisced about past staff outings, and made plans for the upcoming week. Despite the underlying tension about the issues they were facing, the dinner turned into a pleasant gathering, with everyone appreciating the moment of togetherness.

As the meal drew to a close, they felt a renewed sense of unity and resolve. They knew challenges awaited them, but for now they focused on supporting each other and ensuring that Camilla returned to a welcoming home.

Chapter Twenty-One

Late the following afternoon, the doorbell rang. Sally opened the door to find Danny Anderson standing there, visibly troubled. Her eyes widened with excitement and surprise. "Danny! I can't believe it's you!" she exclaimed, stepping aside to let him in. But her excitement quickly shifted to concern as she noticed his expression. "Camilla's not here but she'll be back tonight. What's going on? Are you alright?"

Once inside, Danny hesitated, taking a shaky breath. "I came back because my father passed away." His voice was thick with emotion. "I've missed Middlemoor so much, but after hearing about Mr. and Mrs. Ashworth I know people must blame me. I know the truth has come out—about the affair. I can't stand the thought of everyone thinking I don't care or that I'm hiding."

Sally's face softened with empathy, and she glanced over at Seb, who was standing nearby, taking in the tense atmosphere. He quickly scuttled off, leaving Danny and Sally alone so Danny could speak more freely.

Sally guided him to the kitchen, where they both settled at the table with cups of coffee. Danny's hands trembled as he lifted the cup to his lips, clearly wrestling with his emotions, wanting to make things right. After a few moments of silence, he spoke in a low, pained voice.

"There's something I've never told anyone," he began, his voice barely above a whisper. "I loved her, Sally. I cared about her deeply, but I never meant to hurt anyone, especially Mr. Ashworth. The guilt has been eating away at me since the day I left. And now... now it feels like the worst has happened because of me."

Sally reached out and placed a gentle hand on his. "That's a heavy burden to carry alone. I'm glad you came back to talk. No one wants you to go through this by yourself."

He gave her a small nod. "Thank you. I was afraid of what you'd think of me, of what everyone would think, now that it's all out in the open."

Sally reassured him gently. "We're here for you. Whatever's happened, we just want to support you."

Danny glanced at the door. "I should go before Camilla gets back. I don't know how she'll react to seeing me. I can't risk upsetting her."

"You don't have to leave. Camilla will be so happy to see you. But if you really feel like you need to go, I understand. Just know you're welcome here."

Danny's shoulders relaxed, and he managed a small nod. "Thanks again, Sally. I didn't know if anyone would understand."

As Danny stood to leave and Sally opened the door, Camilla and David's taxi pulled up to the front of the house. Camilla spotted Danny and her face lit up with surprise and joy. Without hesitation, she leapt out of the car and ran over, enveloping him in a huge hug.

"Danny! It's so good to see you!" she exclaimed, beaming. "How's your father? Is he here too?"

Danny, caught off guard, hesitated before saying, "Actually... he passed away. I came back because... well, I needed to be here."

Camilla's face softened. "Oh, Danny, I'm so sorry." She wrapped her arms around him again. "Stay with us. You shouldn't be alone right now."

"I-I'm fine," he stammered. "I've got a room at the hotel down the road."

Camilla scoffed, shaking her head. "Don't be silly! Cancel it and stay here. It's not up for debate." She gave him a pleading look. "Please?"

After a brief pause, Danny finally nodded, a small smile breaking through his sadness. "Alright, I'll stay."

"Perfect!" Camilla exclaimed, her eyes lighting up. "We've missed you so much. It'll be so good to catch up." She squeezed his arm affectionately, making it clear that she was genuinely happy to have him back.

Sally, eager to make Danny feel at home, flashed a smile. "I'll cook your favourite—beef stroganoff."

Danny chuckled, genuinely touched. "That sounds perfect," he replied, and he went to his car to grab his things.

As Danny reached his car, the sound of tyres crunching on gravel caught his attention. A police car pulled up at the front of the driveway, and a ripple of tension moved through the group. Sally's eyes widened, and she quickly exchanged concerned glances with Seb and Danny. The unspoken message was clear—they needed to keep Camilla calm and focused elsewhere.

Seb subtly stepped closer to Camilla, who was still near the door, chatting happily about how nice it was to have Danny staying with them. "Camilla," he said gently, "why don't you come inside? We can start pouring the drinks, and you can tell us more about the holiday."

David, catching on, moved towards the house with a quick nod to Seb, intent on sparing Camilla any further stress. He knew how fragile she'd been, and the last thing they needed was for her to be upset again.

Sally walked briskly over to the police car as Officer Lockwood stepped out. She offered a polite but tense smile, bracing herself for the news. Lockwood's expression was sympathetic as he spoke. "The dental records have come back," he began in a low voice. "They've identified an older woman who was reported missing a few months ago."

A wave of relief washed over Sally—relief that the head wasn't Ben's—but it was mixed with sadness for the woman's family. "Thank you for letting us know," she said quietly, her voice steady despite the emotions swirling inside her.

Lockwood nodded and returned to his car; Sally took a moment to gather herself. Though Ben was still missing, the knowledge the body on the beach wasn't him offered small, fragile hope. She clung to this as she walked back towards the house. Ben could still be out there, and for the moment, that hope was enough to keep her going.

After dinner, the group gathered in the drawing room. Its high ceilings and richly patterned wallpaper gave the space

The Crimes of Middlemoor Estate

an old-world charm. Camilla and David were on the burgundy sofa by the fire, relaxed and content, sharing stories from their recent holiday. Nearby, Sally sipped her wine, her expression calm but with a hint of tension in her eyes, while Sebastian listened with polite interest, a mug of herbal tea in his hands.

Karin casually flipped through a magazine but occasionally glanced up to follow the conversation, her quiet presence a steadying influence. David's gaze shifted to Danny who sat near the window away from the others, his glass of whiskey barely touched. Danny's distant stare hinted at something unresolved.

The absence of Terry was noticeable but not unexpected; he had excused himself after dinner, heading back to the gatehouse to unwind with his usual evening TV shows. The room hummed with quiet conversation until Camilla picked up her phone and broke the tranquillity. "Oh, there was a police presence at Plymouth beach yesterday," she said, her voice calm. "They've identified a washed-up head—an elderly woman. *Tavistock Heritage & Hills* have just posted an article!"

The news dropped into the room like a stone, sending ripples of unease. Sally stiffened, and she exchanged a quick look with Sebastian, though she quickly forced a small smile. "At least the family has some closure," she murmured.

Conversation drifted back to safer topics, but the laughter was subdued.

Finally, Danny spoke, his voice shaky. "Camilla... would it be okay if I came back to Middlemoor?"

The question hung in the air. Danny avoided looking at anyone, instead staring down at his hands, which still held the untouched whiskey.

Camilla didn't hesitate. She leaned forward slightly, her gaze steady and sincere. "Of course, Danny," she said. "Why wouldn't it be okay?" She paused, then added with a smile, "You're always welcome back. It's your home, too, no matter what's happened in the past."

Danny glanced up at her, uncertainty still lingering in his eyes. "But... with everything that's gone on? I mean, it's been so long, and... well, things aren't exactly simple, are they?"

Camilla shook her head, a small laugh escaping her lips. "Don't be daft. That was all a long time ago." Her words were gentle, but her tone carried a weight of finality, as if she were closing the door on old wounds. "Whatever happened before, it's not your burden anymore, Danny. You're part of this place—always have been, always will be. You're family."

There was something about her certainty, the way she made it sound so simple, that settled the knot of hesitation in Danny's chest. He didn't deserve the kind of forgiveness she was offering, but in that moment, he felt it, as though it were a gift he hadn't expected but desperately needed.

"Thanks," he muttered, his voice thick with emotion. "I... I don't know what to say."

"No need to say anything," Camilla replied with a smile. "Just come back and be yourself. We'll take care of the rest."

Sally, who had been watching quietly from across the room, spoke up, her voice light but pointed. "I think we could all use some fresh air around here, Danny. Middlemoor's not the same without you."

Danny gave her a small smile. The group wasn't perfect, and there were still a lot of things left unsaid, but in that moment, he realised that perhaps returning to Middlemoor wasn't as impossible as he'd once thought.

Karin finally spoke up, her voice soft but sincere. "It's

true. It's not the same when someone's missing. You bring something to Middlemoor, Danny. Don't forget that."

Danny looked over at her, and for the first time that evening, a flicker of happiness crossed his features. "Thanks, Karin," he muttered.

Sebastian shot Danny a smirk, eyes glinting with mischief. "Just so you know, I've missed you the most," he said, voice low and daring, holding Danny's gaze a beat too long, his expression unmistakably suggestive. Danny rolled his eyes, but a faint blush crept up, and he suddenly felt like he was home once again.

Chapter Twenty-Two

That weekend, on Saturday morning, four urban explorers set out on a journey along the abandoned railway line that once connected Ivybridge and Tavistock. The track skirted the edges of the village of Middlemoor, which, despite its proximity to the line, never had a functioning train station. Passenger numbers dwindled in the late 1950s, leading to its eventual closure. As the explorers pressed on, they approached a section where the track wound through the hills and into a long-forgotten tunnel leading towards Tavistock. This two-mile tunnel, sealed off for safety reasons since the closure, had become a magnet for thrill-seekers and YouTubers eager to capture the eerie atmosphere of abandoned places. Local legend claimed that the ghostly sound of phantom trains could still be heard echoing through the hills. Enticed by these tales, the four explorers had travelled all the way from the US, determined to uncover the mysteries buried within the tunnel.

Jonah, one of the group, knelt down and rummaged through his bag, pulling out the tools he'd brought for the task. The entrance to the tunnel on the Middlemoor side was stubbornly secured, but with some effort he managed to pry it open. The weathered boards bore the scars of previous intrusions, evidence that others had attempted—and succeeded—in breaking in before, only for the entrance to be sealed up again each time.

Ignoring the numerous warning signs that screamed *Danger* and *No Entry*, Jonah, Corey, Ava, and Brielle steeled themselves and stepped into the tunnel, their torches flickering to life. With a mix of unease and determination, they ventured deeper into the tunnel.

"Make sure you're getting this, Corey," Jonah whispered, glancing back at his friend who was filming their progress. "The viewers are gonna love this. Talk about the perfect spooky set-up!"

Corey nodded, the camera capturing the wet moss-covered walls as they ventured further into the darkness. "Already got it, man. This is going to blow up."

Ava, holding the microphone close to her mouth, spoke quietly. "We've just entered the abandoned rail tunnel, and it's already living up to the legends. It's dark, damp, and totally creepy—exactly what we were hoping for."

Brielle, the designated editor, glanced at Ava with a hint of nervous excitement. "Imagine the reactions when they see this part. No one's gonna believe we actually went through with it."

They pressed on, the surroundings remaining unchanged until they reached a point roughly halfway through where they encountered a small platform resembling a fire escape. Its curved top created an overhang. As they approached, their torches revealed a figure lying under the platform in a seemingly peaceful sleep. The sight startled them, and unease settled over the group. They wondered why someone would be sleeping in the middle of an abandoned tunnel.

"Are you guys seeing this?" Corey whispered, the camera zooming in on the figure. "This... this doesn't feel right."

"Hello?" Jonah called out, his voice echoing through the darkness.

There was a moment of silence, and the figure remained still.

"Hiiiii," Ava tried again, her voice uncertain.

"We should check on them," Brielle suggested, lowering her camera. "They might be ill and in need of help."

With growing concern, they carefully approached the figure, their torches casting shadows on the walls as they moved closer.

"Corey, keep filming," Jonah instructed. "We need to document this in case they need help—or worse."

As they drew closer, the flickering torchlight revealed a horrifying truth. The figure wasn't merely asleep; it was a decomposing body, sunken and far beyond any help. Shocked and terrified, the group turned and ran, the camera still recording as they fled. The return journey, which had seemed lengthy on the way in, was now swift as they raced towards the daylight.

When they emerged, Jonah fumbled for his phone and dialled 911.

"It's not connecting!" he exclaimed in frustration.

"Did you dial 999? We're in the UK, remember?" Corey pointed out.

"Oh, right! Of course."

It wasn't long before the police arrived. DS Ransome stepped out of the squad car and approached them.

"I understand you've found a body," he said. "Due to

health and safety regulations, I can't have you show me where the body is directly as it's potentially a crime scene. But I need an exact location."

"It's about halfway in," Jonah explained. "There's a small platform—kind of like a fire escape. The body's underneath it. At first, we thought it was someone sleeping, but it's definitely not."

"Alright, thank you. We'll suit up with safety gear and head in. I'll need you to stay with one of my colleagues until we've reached the body. We need to ensure we locate it before you can leave. My colleague will then take you back to your home or hotel, wherever you're staying. Are you all okay?"

"Yes, thank you," Jonah replied. "Just a bit shaken. It wasn't what we expected. We have it all on film. Obviously, we won't be using it for our social media, so you're welcome to it."

Jonah handed over the memory card, and Ransome nodded, taking it carefully as his team prepared for the recovery operation.

Following the directions provided by Jonah, Ransome and two other officers arrived at the location quickly. As Ransome approached, he noticed an unusual odour, less intense than that of a recently deceased body, suggesting the corpse had been there for some time.

He carefully looked over the body using his flashlight to illuminate it. Although he couldn't make a definitive identification until further examinations were completed, the clothing matched what Ben was last seen wearing on the CCTV footage.

Ransome paused, a frown creasing his brow. "Hang on, what's this?" He scanned the surrounding area.

He took out his radio, his heart racing as he processed the significance of what he had found.

"All units, I can confirm that we have located the body and something else... I need the area investigated by scene of crime officers immediately."

With his team in charge of carefully transporting the body to the hospital mortuary near Plymouth for examination, Ransome set out for Camilla's residence, steeling himself for the difficult conversation ahead. The feeling that all was not as it seemed lingered in his gut, leaving him unsettled as he prepared to deliver the grim news.

Camilla, already sensing the gravity of the moment, clutched a tissue in one hand and held tightly to David with the other. Tears silently streamed down her face. She didn't need to hear the words to know what was coming—Ransome's solemn expression said it all.

Ransome took a deep breath, as he met Camilla's tearful gaze. He hesitated for a moment, carefully choosing his words.

"Camilla, everyone... I'm afraid I have some difficult news," he began, his voice gentle but firm. "Earlier today, a group of urban explorers discovered a body in the old rail tunnel. While I can't officially confirm the identity yet, the clothing found on the body matches what Ben was wearing the day he went missing."

Camilla gasped, her hand tightening around David's. "Are you sure?" she whispered, her voice trembling.

Ransome shook his head slightly. "I can't be certain until the post-mortem is completed and identification is confirmed but based on the description of the clothes... it's very likely. I wanted to come here and tell you in person before the news spread."

David nodded, trying to remain composed. "What happens now?"

"The body has been taken to the mortuary for a formal identification process," Ransome explained. "I'll keep you informed every step of the way. I'm so sorry that I can't give you a definitive answer right now."

Camilla's tears flowed freely, and she leaned into David, who wrapped an arm around her. "Thank you for telling us," David said quietly. "Please... just keep us updated."

"I will," Ransome assured them. "And if there's anything else you need, don't hesitate to reach out. I'm truly sorry for what you're going through."

Camilla looked up at Ransome and, her voice shaky but determined, asked, "Could you tell what happened to the person? Was there any sign of... how they might have died?"

Ransome sighed, his expression mournful as he tried to convey the uncertainty of the situation. "I wish I could give you a clear answer, Camilla. Right now, though, we can't be sure until further investigation is done. The pathologist will need to conduct a thorough post-mortem to determine the cause of death."

"But... was there anything at the scene that could give us a clue?"

Ransome hesitated, then spoke carefully. "We found some tools near the body—tools that don't seem to belong in this area. It appears this person may have trapped themself inside, which raises the possibility that this could be a suicide. Of course, we can't confirm anything yet. Given the circumstances and the location, it's a consideration, but we won't know for certain until the investigation is complete."

Camilla's breath caught in her throat and she closed her eyes, trying to process the information. David tightened his grip on her hand, his face etched with concern.

"We'll do everything we can to find out what happened," Ransome added gently. "I promise you that."

All everyone could do was nod.

Chapter Twenty-Three

Within two weeks, the investigation, post-mortem, and forensic examinations were completed, confirming that the body found in the tunnel was indeed Ben. The results also brought a disturbing revelation: Ben's death was not a suicide or accident.

DS Ransome pored over the latest findings. The post-mortem revealed extensive trauma, including broken bones and severe injuries, alongside a shard of knife embedded in his ribs. More alarmingly, the tools found near the body, initially thought to have been used to block the entrance, bore fingerprints that did not match Ben's or any known individuals in the database. This pointed to the involvement of another person during Ben's final moments.

Ransome needed to speak with Camilla and share the grim news that would shatter whatever semblance of peace she had found since the tragedy. He picked up his radio. "I'm heading to Camilla's residence. Prepare for a detailed briefing."

The drive to her home felt interminable. Upon arriving at the grand estate, he noticed the drawn curtains and the stillness that enveloped the house. He knocked gently, apprehension coursing through him.

Camilla opened the door, her eyes red and swollen. "DS Ransome," she said, her voice barely above a whisper as she stepped aside.

"Camilla," he replied, adopting a tone of compassion. "We need to talk."

They settled in the drawing room, where framed photographs of Ben lined the walls, stark reminders of happier times now overshadowed by grief. Camilla sat on the edge of a plush armchair, her hands clenched in her lap.

"Ransome, I thought maybe..." she began, struggling to find her voice. "I hoped for some closure."

Ransome took a moment, carefully choosing his words. "I wish I could offer that, but the investigation has revealed some troubling details. The autopsy confirmed that Ben's death was not self-inflicted nor accidental."

Her expression shifted, confusion etched across her face. "What do you mean?"

"There were signs of a struggle. The tools we found near his body have fingerprints that don't match his, indicating that someone else was there. This suggests foul play."

Camilla's face drained of colour, and fresh tears spilled down her cheeks. "So, someone killed him? Why? Who would do such a thing?"

"We're still working to uncover who it was and the motive, but we need to investigate anyone who had access to that area or a reason to harm him." Ransome leaned forward, his gaze steady. "I know this is a lot to process, but we will do our utmost to find out the truth."

"How could this happen?" she whispered, the enormity of the situation crashing down on her. "I can't believe that he—"

"Camilla," he interrupted gently, "you're not alone in this. I'm committed to finding justice for Ben."

She wiped her tears, taking a shaky breath to compose herself. "I want to honour his memory, but I feel so lost right now. How do I even start?"

"Take it one step at a time," Ransome said. "It's okay to grieve and to feel overwhelmed. Just know that we will pursue every lead."

Ransome left Middlemoor Estate with a heavy heart but a determined spirit.

As the months rolled on, the investigation stagnated. Each day brought new disappointments; no fresh leads emerged, leaving the police grasping at straws. Despite their exhaustive efforts, there was no indication of who was involved in Ben's death or what could have motivated such a brutal act. The absence of answers was deeply unsettling. With each passing day, uncertainty pressed down on Camilla, yet she knew she couldn't let her life remain suspended in grief and confusion forever.

Eventually, Camilla faced a painful truth: she needed to find a way to move forward and release the burdens that threatened to drag her down. Although Ben was gone, and the search for answers persisted, she clung to the hope that at least knowing his fate could bring her some measure of peace. The local area, once a reassuring backdrop to her life with Ben, now felt stifling, suffused with reminders of her loss. Yet, in spite of the discomfort that filled every familiar space, she resolved to keep the estate. The house represented more than mere bricks and mortar; it was a testament to their life together and a sanctuary of cherished memories.

With steadfast resolve, Camilla dedicated herself to preserving Middlemoor Estate, ensuring it would flourish as a tribute to Ben's spirit. With the unwavering support of David and the staff, who had become invaluable allies, she worked tirelessly to breathe new life into their home. They spent late nights filled with laughter and creative planning, pouring their energy into transforming the estate into a vibrant hub that honoured the memories of Ben and his parents.

Through this collective effort, Camilla discovered a renewed sense of purpose amidst her sorrow. Each step she took became a tribute to the love they had shared, a way to honour Ben's legacy while forging a new path for herself. With David by her side, she felt a flicker of hope igniting within her—a belief that, although the road ahead would be fraught with challenges, she could thrive and build a future infused with the love and spirit of the man she had lost. Together, they would navigate the uncertainties of their new reality, committed to ensuring that the story of Middlemoor Estate would continue, filled with the laughter and warmth that Ben would have wanted for her.

TAVISTOCK HERITAGE & HILLS

Police Confirm Identity of Body Found in Middlemoor Tunnel as Ben Ashworth and Reveal Shocking New Evidence

The tragic discovery in Middlemoor's abandoned railway tunnel has taken a dark turn. Police confirmed this week that the body found by American YouTubers last month was indeed that of Ben Ashworth, a local man missing for over a year. However, forensic examinations now indicate that Ashworth's death was not an accident or suicide, but a violent crime.

Detective Sergeant Ransome, the detective leading the investigation, released details from the post-mortem: Ashworth suffered multiple injuries, including broken bones and stab wounds. Adding to the mystery, fingerprints found on tools at the scene do not match Ashworth or any individuals in police records.

"This is a distressing revelation,"

Ransome said. "The fingerprints and evidence of a struggle strongly point to foul play. We're determined to track down who was with Ben in his final moments and bring justice for his family."

The news has shattered any remaining hope of closure for Ashworth's family, particularly his wife, Camilla, who, devastated by the findings, said, "I can't understand how anyone could do this to him. We need answers."

Camilla, who faced early suspicion in her husband's disappearance, has consistently cooperated with investigators and was recently described by police as "not connected to any wrongdoing." Yet, in a close-knit community like Tavistock, whispers and speculation about her role—once fuelled by her reserved demeanour—have been difficult to silence.

Police have issued a call for information, seeking any witnesses who might have noticed unusual activity near the abandoned tunnel or who had seen Ashworth before he vanished. Despite exhaustive investigative efforts, leads have been scarce, and the case remains unsolved.

Chapter Twenty-Four

Ten years later

As the morning sun filtered through the kitchen window, casting a glow over the room, Camilla hummed a tune while sitting at the table surrounded by paperwork and her laptop. The scent of freshly baked bread and sizzling bacon filled the air as Sally prepared breakfast. Just then, the patter of little feet echoed in the hallway.

"Mum! Mum!" came the excited voices of her twin boys, Felix and Artie, as they bounded into the kitchen. Their identical faces were flushed with excitement, their crystal-blue eyes sparkling with anticipation.

"Good morning, my little adventurers." Camilla greeted them with a smile. "What's the excitement all about?"

Felix, always the spokesperson for the duo, stepped

forward. "Mum, can we go out into the grounds and explore the gardens?"

"Are the radios charged up?" Camilla asked.

"Yeah, they are!" Felix smiled while checking both radios.

Artie, slightly shyer but equally eager, nodded enthusiastically. "Please, Mum?"

Camilla looked at her boys, their eager faces brimming with innocence and curiosity. She couldn't help but chuckle. The twins had recently developed a fascination with the sprawling grounds surrounding their home, a world that promised endless adventures.

"Alright, you two," she said. "But first, you need to eat your breakfast. Exploring takes a lot of energy, you know."

Sally placed their breakfasts down along with glasses of orange juice. The boys cheered, thanked Sally and quickly took their seats at the table, their little legs swinging with excitement as they devoured their meal. Between bites, they talked about the treasures they hoped to find and the imaginary creatures they might encounter.

When they finished, Camilla handed them their backpacks, each one packed with snacks, water, and a little notebook for their discoveries. "Stay together and be careful," she reminded them gently. "If you're taking your bikes, keep your helmets on and don't go beyond the big oak tree. Remember, it's easy to get lost."

"We will, Mum!" Felix promised, handing Camilla one of the radios. "Come on, Artie!"

Camilla watched as her sons dashed out the door, their laughter echoing through the morning air. She followed them to the porch and stood for a moment, her heart filled with a mix of

The Crimes of Middlemoor Estate

pride and a hint of worry. The garden, with its winding paths and hidden corners, was a place of magic and mystery for the twins. She knew that every flower they discovered and every bug they observed was a step on their journey of growing up. As she watched them disappear into the greenery, she whispered up to the clouds for their safety, trusting in their bond and sense of adventure to guide them. With a sigh, Camilla turned back to her chores, the sound of her boys' laughter still lingering in the air, a sweet reminder of the simple childhood joys.

David had spent the past week in London on business for W&A, and as his taxi approached the front of Middlemoor Estate, relief washed over him. The sprawling estate, with its rolling green lawns and ancient oak trees, looked especially inviting after the hustle and bustle of city life. He stepped out of the car, stretched and took a deep breath of fresh country air. It just smelt so clean and healthy.

Camilla was waiting for him at the front door, a bright smile lighting up her face. She had missed him terribly, and the days seemed to drag without his presence. As he walked up the steps, she rushed to him, wrapping her arms around his neck in an embrace.

"Welcome home, darling!" she exclaimed, her eyes sparkling with excitement.

"It's good to be back, Mrs O'Sullivan," David replied, kissing her gently. "How have things been here?"

"Busy," Camilla said, a hint of mischief in her voice. "But

I have something exciting to discuss with you. Let's go inside."

Curious, David followed her into the grand foyer, where the smell of Sally's freshly baked bread wafted through the air. They made their way to the cosy sitting room, where a fire crackled and a small breakfast platter along with a fresh teapot sat looking very inviting. David sank into his favourite armchair while Camilla perched on the edge of the sofa, her eyes twinkling with anticipation.

"What's the big news? There seems to be a lot of paperwork involved. Should I be worried?" David asked, intrigued but also slightly nervous.

"Well," Camilla began, "I've been thinking about Middlemoor and how beautiful it is. I believe it has the potential to be a fantastic wedding venue!"

David raised an eyebrow, surprised but intrigued by the idea. "A wedding venue? Here?"

"Yes," Camilla said, nodding enthusiastically. "I know it's had a dark past, not the best media coverage but despite all that, we have the perfect setting. The gardens, the ballroom, the picturesque views—it's all so romantic. I think couples would love to get married here. It could be a project for us all to work on."

Just then, Sebastian burst into the room, his face beaming. "Did I hear something about a wedding venue?"

"Oh, Sebastian, like you haven't been a big part of this idea..." David chuckled while pouring a cuppa.

"I can help organise everything—the flowers, decor, the music. I already have so many ideas." Seb whipped out his pink notebook and fluffy pen.

Camilla laughed, clearly delighted by Seb's contribution to roping David in. "See, David? We are all on board here.

And we have plenty of rooms to offer should people want to stay the night of the wedding. It'll be so much fun. Ward & Ashworth is as successful as ever, especially with how you run it, and you don't need me dabbling in it anymore so I would love a new thing to start. Open our home to the world and show them just how perfect the gorgeous grounds are."

David looked at Camilla and Seb, their faces glowing with possibilities. He thought about the quiet elegance of Middlemoor, the serenity it offered, and how it could indeed be the perfect backdrop for couples starting their lives together.

"Alright," he said finally, a smile spreading across his face. "Let's do it. Let's turn Middlemoor into a wedding venue!"

Camilla clapped her hands in delight, and Sebastian let out a whoop of joy, immediately launching into a detailed list of plans and ideas. As David listened to them talk, he felt a warmth in his heart. Middlemoor was not just a home; it was a place where dreams could come true. And with his family by his side, he knew they could make anything happen.

Felix and Artie were still out exploring. They had ended up past the big old oak tree without realising. Felix noticed an owl with piercing golden eyes perched on a branch. Its gaze was unyielding, and Felix felt a strange connection, as if the bird was calling to them.

"Artie, do you see that?" Felix whispered, pointing to the owl.

Artie nodded, his curiosity piqued. The owl hooted softly and took flight, circling their heads before flying off towards a denser part of the woods. The boys exchanged a glance, a silent agreement passing between them, and they decided to follow.

The owl led them deeper into the woods than they had ever ventured before, to a clearing surrounded by gnarled trees. In the centre of the clearing, hidden by overgrown vines and brambles, was an old stone well. The owl perched on the edge, staring at the boys with an intensity that sent shivers down their spines.

"Do you think this is what it wanted us to find?" Artie asked, his voice barely above a whisper.

Felix nodded, stepping closer to the well. He brushed away the vines, revealing the moss-covered stones. There was a wooden bucket and a frayed rope, long unused. Curiosity overcoming caution, Felix peered over the edge, but all he could see was darkness. There was an old rusty ladder leading into the dark.

"Do you have a torch?" Felix asked.

"Yes, I think so. In my backpack." Artie reached for it.

Shining the torch down, they saw there was no water. It just looked muddy.

Despite the danger, the boys were determined to go down. They slowly climbed over the edge of the stone wall onto the ladder and slowly descended into the well, the air growing colder with each step. The walls were damp and covered in slick thick moss. Finally, reaching the bottom, their feet touched solid ground, and they found themselves in a cavernous chamber. Using the torch, they illuminated their surroundings. The faint light revealed nothing but a bundled sheet of some sort. It was dirty but you could just about see the sheet had owls on it. Felix wandered over to get a closer look. Being the more confident one, he pulled at the sheet. As he began to unwrap it, the torchlight exposed something horrifying—a skeleton!

"Is it real?" Artie asked worryingly.

"I don't know." Felix stepped back and grabbed the radio. "Mum? Mum?" he called but they were too far away for a connection.

Chapter Twenty-Five

The twins burst through the back door, their faces pale and eyes wide with shock. Camilla and David looked up from their coffee, sensing immediately that something was wrong.

"What's happened? Are you boys alright?" Camilla asked, rushing over to them.

"M-mum, we f-found something," Artie stammered, his voice trembling. "At the bottom of an old well in the woods."

"What well? What are you talking about?" David asked, a puzzled look on his face.

"Bones, Dad. Human bones," Felix added, his voice shaking.

Camilla's face blanched as she absorbed their words. Without a moment's hesitation, she grabbed the phone and called the police. Within minutes, the tranquil scene around their secluded home was shattered by the arrival of emergency services, again!

The boys led everyone to the hidden well. Camilla was

annoyed as it was clearly past the old oak tree but now wasn't the time to tell the boys off.

The family and staff gathered near the well, a place no one knew about. Camilla held David's hand tightly, drawing strength from her husband's presence. They exchanged a look, silently bracing themselves for whatever lay ahead.

Karin came running from a golf buggy, having rushed over as soon as she got Camilla's frantic call. She enveloped Camilla in a tight hug before turning her attention to the boys.

"Come on, you two. Let's get you away from here," she said gently, steering the twins towards the buggy. "You don't need to see this."

Camilla watched them go, then turned back towards the well where the police and emergency responders were working diligently. They had already started to hoist something up—something large, wrapped in bedding decorated with an owl pattern that was familiar. Her heart pounded in her chest as she slowly recognised the decayed fabric.

"That's the missing bedding from my mother's room," she whispered, her voice trembling.

"We'll need to examine the remains, but from the initial look, we believe the skeleton is female. The long hair around the skull suggests that."

Camilla's legs felt weak, and she leaned into David for support. They stood together, watching as the skeleton was carefully placed on a stretcher and carried away. She felt a fresh wave of grief and confusion wash over her. Who was this woman, and how had she ended up at the bottom of their well in her mother's missing bedding?

The questions swirled in her mind, but all she could do was wait for answers. David squeezed her hand.

"We'll get through this," he murmured, his voice filled with quiet determination.

Camilla nodded.

Later that evening, when everyone had gone to bed, the old stone well stood under the silvery veil of moonlight. Earlier, the scene had been bustling with activity, but now it was back to being a lonely place, surrounded by eerie stillness.

Resting on the edge of the well was the owl, its feathers glistening. She had been a silent observer throughout the day's events, her amber eyes reflecting the sorrow and relief that, after a decade, the skeleton had finally been found.

Spreading her wings to take flight into the night sky, a haunting question lingered: who was this dedicated sentinel? Though the bird had the body of a beast, her soul was that of a devoted mother. She had waited for years to lead someone to her human form, and finally the mission was realised.

Having fulfilled her silent vigil, she could now depart. As she soared into the sky, her shadow cast long and lean against the ground and a sense of peace settled over the well. The owl's departure signalled the end of an era, a final goodbye to a watchful guardian. In the quiet embrace of the night, Caroline's spirit was finally set free.

Chapter Twenty-Six

Almost 500 miles away, Richard sat alone in a dimly lit pub on the outskirts of Edinburgh, a place as desolate as his own life had become. It had been over a decade since his father had thrown him out, but the memory lingered, sharp and painful, as if it had happened only yesterday. With hindsight, he realised it had been inevitable. The warnings had been clear, repeated time and again, but he had shrugged them off, thinking his mother's love would shield him from the worst. He couldn't have been more wrong.

Mr. Coldwell's pleas had fallen on deaf ears, and he had reached breaking point. Desperate and fearing for their family, he had confided in his wife, knowing the truth would devastate her but hoping it might finally push Richard to change. Her reaction, however, was even worse than he had imagined. The idealised image she held of her son was obliterated, replaced by the harsh reality of his addiction. The confrontation that ensued was explosive, tearing their family apart in a single night of rage and anguish. Unable to reconcile the son she had cherished with the addict he had become, his mother, heartbroken and overwhelmed, made the painful decision to cut him off completely. The wounds left behind were deep, and the family, once whole, was shattered beyond repair.

Since then, he had lost track of his parents' lives, though the familiar shortbread still lined the shelves of every shop, a bittersweet reminder of the life he once had. Richard's own life had taken a darker turn. He was now entangled in the grim underworld of Edinburgh, running drugs to make ends meet. Nights were spent on the streets or in cheap hostels, numbing his pain with whatever drugs and alcohol he could afford. He was friendless, drowning in depression, and regularly found himself on the receiving end of beatings. No one from his past had tried to find him, a stark testament to the person he had become in their eyes.

He stared into the half-empty pint of ale in front of him, his fingers curled around the glass. It wasn't his first drink of the day, and it probably wouldn't be his last. His mind wandered as he listened to the murmur of conversations around him, the clink of glasses, and the music from the old jukebox in the corner. It was a place where one could easily disappear, and that suited Richard just fine.

His attention was drawn to the television as the news anchor's voice grew louder, the tinny sound carrying across the pub. The image on the screen shifted to a remote location: the rolling estate of Middlemoor.

"The skeletal remains of an unidentified individual were discovered yesterday in an old well on the Middlemoor Estate," the anchor reported, her tone even. "The grim find was made by the property owner's two children. The estate, as many will recall, is steeped in troubled history, most infamously associated with the notorious Ashworth family. Given the estate's dark past, authorities are now investigating the possibility of foul play."

Richard gripped his drink and took a deep breath.

"Authorities have yet to confirm the identity of the remains," the anchor continued, "but sources suggest they may date back a decade. The discovery has reignited interest in the estate, long the focus of speculation and conspiracy theories spanning generations."

Richard felt the room begin to spin, his vision blurring as cold sweat clung to his skin. His heart raced, a dull thudding in his chest that threatened to drown out the murmurs and chatter around him. He needed to leave—now. He pushed himself up from the bar stool, but his legs wobbled beneath him, nearly giving way as he staggered to his feet.

"Stumbling already, Richard?" a voice chimed mockingly from across the room. "Bit early in the day for that, don't you think?" It was one of the regulars; his grin was wide and full of malice but Richard barely registered it. The sound was distant, like it was being filtered through thick cotton.

He didn't respond, couldn't respond, as he made his way to the door. He fumbled with the handle, and when he finally pushed it open, the brisk cool air slammed into him, waking his senses for the first time in what felt like hours. He stepped outside and inhaled deeply, gasping as if he had been underwater too long. The air filled his lungs, momentarily clearing the fog from his mind. But the clarity came with a heavy weight—the weight of his guilt, of the unspeakable things he had done.

Was it time to confess? Could he really admit that he was behind the deaths of Benedict and Caroline? His stomach churned at the thought. He hadn't physically been the one to do it, but that didn't matter, did it? He had orchestrated everything, pulling strings from behind the scenes with the cold detachment of a puppet master. And with money his father had assumed was being squandered on drugs. To some degree, Mr. Coldwell had been right, but Richard had sunk far deeper than that.

The drugs had served as a mask, a smokescreen for the real operation: the hitmen, the bribes, the forged documents. Richard had paid for it all with his father's wealth, money that only someone of their status would have access to. Everything had been meticulously planned, especially Caroline's death: the fake doctor call, the counterfeit death certificate, even the false ashes. No one had suspected a thing. They were none the wiser to the truth that the deaths of Benedict and Caroline had been paid for with blood money.

But now? Now, Richard could barely hold himself together. His life had unravelled, piece by piece, until all that was left was a shell of a man. He was constantly on edge, and plagued by paranoia and regret. His once comfortable existence had devolved into a waking nightmare, and the insignificance of it all was crushing him. What had it all been for? What had he gained? The money was gone, and with it, his peace of mind.

He leaned against the wall of the pub and stared out at the empty street. What if he turned himself in? What if he went to the police and admitted everything? It wasn't like he had much left to lose. His life had become a hollow, miserable thing: his every waking moment filled with dread; his every night spent haunted by nightmares. Prison would be an escape, in a way. At least there he'd have a bed, a hot meal. Stability. Maybe even some semblance of safety.

And maybe, just maybe, his parents would visit him. That thought lingered for a moment longer than it should, the twisted hope that somehow, after everything, they might still care enough to see him.

Screw it, Richard thought, blinking through the haze that still clouded his vision. Everything around him felt distorted, like he was watching the world through thick fog.

"Excuse me, do you know where the nearest police station is?" he asked an elderly couple who were passing by.

The man paused, a hint of concern creeping into his expression. "Yeah, mate, but it's a bit of a walk. Everything alright?"

"Uh, yeah." Richard hesitated, then added, "I just need to go... confess something."

The couple exchanged glances. A flicker of unease crossed their faces.

"Here," the man said, handing Richard a twenty-pound note. "Let me call you a taxi."

Richard shook his head, pushing the money back. "No, really. I can't take that. You don't want to help me. I'm... I'm a terrible person."

The man regarded him for a moment, then nodded softly. "Maybe so, but you're trying to make it right. That counts for something."

The woman gave a gentle smile, and before Richard could protest further, the man was already on the phone. Within minutes, a taxi pulled up, but the couple had quietly slipped away, leaving Richard alone on the kerb with the crumpled twenty-pound note in his hand.

"Taxi for the police station?" the driver called, rolling down her window.

Richard swallowed hard. "Yeah. Please."

As the sun dipped below the horizon, the streets darkened, casting long shadows. The ride to the station felt unnervingly short—like time had sped up, compressing his anxiety into a tight knot in his chest.

"That'll be fifteen pounds forty-five," the driver said as they came to a stop. She glanced at Richard with mild scepticism, as if she didn't expect him to pay. His clothes were rumpled, and there was a faint sour smell about him.

But Richard surprised her. He handed over the twenty-pound note and said, "Keep the change."

They exchanged a brief smile before he got out of the taxi. As he walked towards the station doors, a strange calmness settled over him. For the first time in years, he felt like the weight he'd been carrying might finally be lifted.

Richard stepped inside, a strange mix of confidence and dread coming over him as he approached the reception desk. The woman behind it offered a polite smile.

"Good evening. How can I help you?" she asked.

"Hi, uh, I'm here to make a confession," Richard said, his voice steady, though he could feel his pulse quickening.

Her expression faltered for a moment, but she quickly regained her composure. "Oh, I see. Please give me a moment. I'll get an officer for you."

After a brief wait, a tall, sharply dressed officer approached him. His presence commanded attention.

"Good evening, I'm Detective Constable Banks. I understand you're here to confess to a crime?" His tone was calm but serious. "Would you follow me, please?"

"Yes, thank you," Richard replied.

He followed Detective Constable Banks into a small sterile room. A single table sat in the middle, surrounded by a few metal chairs. It felt suffocating, the kind of room where the truth couldn't be avoided.

"I'll need to record this conversation if that's alright with you," Banks said, gesturing to a small recorder.

"Yes, I understand."

Banks pressed the record button. "Can you tell me why you're here tonight?"

Richard hesitated for a second, then began. "Over ten years ago, I hired someone... to get rid of my best friend. He had taken something from me—a girl. Not that I even cared for her that much, at least not in the way it sounds. But I was different back then and a drug addict. Nobody took anything from me. I was the spoiled son of a billionaire. I had it all."

He swallowed hard, the memories flashing before his eyes. "I cheated on her, so she left me and ended up with him —my 'best friend'. They got married and it ate at me. I was bitter, angry, and I heard about people you could hire... people who could make others disappear. I wanted to hurt her so much that I didn't just stop at him. I went after her mother, too. That's whose body they've found in Middlemoor."

Detective Constable Banks held up a hand, his face serious. "I need to stop you there, Richard. Are you telling me that the body found in a well on Middlemoor Estate is connected to you?"

Richard nodded slowly. "Yes. It's all connected to me. I've kept these secrets for years... all to hurt one person. And now... I need to confess."

Detective Constable Banks took a deep breath, his face set in grim resolve. "That's enough for now. Richard, I'm placing you under arrest. You do not have to say anything, but it may harm your defence if you do not mention, when questioned, something which you later rely on in court. Anything you do say may be given in evidence."

As Banks snapped the handcuffs on his wrists, Richard felt a hollow relief. The burden he had carried for so long was finally out in the open.

He was led down a corridor to a small dimly lit cell. Inside, there was nothing but a hard bed, a toilet, and a sink.

Richard sat on the edge of the bed, staring at the floor. The hours dragged by until the first light of dawn crept in through the narrow window.

Chapter Twenty-Seven

Richard had just drifted off when Banks entered the cell and stirred him from a restless sleep. His bloodshot eyes, heavy with exhaustion, blinked open as he looked up at the officer.

"Richard," Banks said gently, "we have a police vehicle outside. It'll take you to Plymouth station where Detective Sergeant Ransome will be waiting for you."

Richard rubbed his face, trying to clear his mind.

"Follow me," Banks continued, holding out a neatly folded prison uniform. "You can take a shower and change into these. But make it quick—we've got a long drive ahead of us."

Richard nodded, and rose stiffly from the bed as Banks led him to the shower facilities.

Ten minutes later, freshly showered and dressed in the plain prison uniform, Richard was escorted outside. The sky above was a dull grey as he was guided into the waiting police vehicle, the long journey back to Plymouth—and to his reckoning—just beginning.

The journey from Edinburgh to Plymouth felt endless, the sound of the engine the only constant as the police vehicle cut through the countryside. Richard sat alone in the back, his wrists cuffed loosely in front of him, staring blankly out of the window. The landscape shifted from the rolling hills of Scotland to the flat, barren stretches of northern England, but it all blurred together. Time had lost meaning. Every so often, the vehicle hit a bump in the road, jostling him from his thoughts, but there was no escaping the heaviness settling in his chest. Guilt, regret, and an aching sense of inevitability gnawed at him. He tried to sleep but couldn't; every time he closed his eyes, memories of the past—the choices, the mistakes—flooded back. The day stretched endlessly, the occasional flicker of passing cars the only reminder that the world outside was still moving, even as his life came to a slow, grinding halt.

Eventually, the vehicle slowed and pulled off the motorway into a petrol station. Richard blinked, momentarily disoriented by the sudden shift in movement. The officers up front exchanged a few quiet words before one stepped out to refuel. The air was cool as the door opened, and Richard could feel a faint breeze slip through the narrow crack of the window. His limbs were stiff from hours of sitting, and he shifted uncomfortably in the back seat, desperate for a stretch.

One of the officers opened the door and looked down at

Richard. "We've got a few minutes if you want to stretch your legs. Just stay close."

Richard nodded, then got out of the vehicle cautiously. His muscles ached as he straightened up, the pavement beneath his feet grounding him in the moment. He glanced around—the station was quiet, almost eerie in the stillness of the afternoon. The only sound came from the petrol pump and the distant cars from the motorway. For a brief moment, Richard let his shoulders relax, inhaling deeply, trying to ignore the situation he was currently in.

But the moment was fleeting. With a silent nod from the officer, he climbed back into the car, the door closing with a solid thud. The journey resumed, and the long road to Plymouth stretched endlessly ahead.

By the time they reached Plymouth, it was nearing 5 p.m. The police vehicle pulled into the station car park, and through the window, Richard spotted a figure waiting at the entrance. His pulse quickened as he guessed this must be Detective Sergeant Ransome. One of the escorting officers opened the door for Richard, and he got out.

"Good afternoon, Richard," the man at the entrance said, his voice steady but commanding. "I'm Detective Sergeant Ransome. I led the investigation into Benedict Ashworth's case."

The mention of his best friend's name sent a shiver down Richard's spine. The past he had tried to bury was now standing right in front of him, demanding to be faced.

"This way, officers," Ransome said, taking hold of Richard's arm as he guided them into the station and down a sterile corridor to an interview room.

"That will be all, officers. You can stand down now," Ransome said, shaking hands with the officers before they left, leaving Richard alone with him in the small claustrophobic room.

Ransome took a seat across from Richard, his gaze sharp and unreadable. "Alright, Richard," he began, flipping open a file. "I understand you're involved in a serious crime. I've listened to the recording, and just so you know, this conversation is also being recorded." His tone was firm but not unkind. "I know it's been a long day, but we'll get through this as quickly as we can so you can rest. I just need to ask you a few questions—about what you said about the case involving Benedict Ashworth, and, of course, Caroline."

Each name he mentioned felt like a punch to Richard's gut, the weight of his confession growing heavier with every passing second.

"What made you want to get rid of Ben in the first place?"

"He took Camilla from me."

"But as I understand it, Camilla had left you after you cheated on her."

"That's true, but my plan was always to win her back."

"Alright, and what steps did you take to try to get her back?"

"I couldn't do much because by the time I realised, they had already started talking. Their relationship grew quickly, and I found out later how close they had become. I was jealous, angry, hurt... I couldn't handle it. From the outside, it might have seemed like I cared more than I actually did, but I was a completely different person back then. I didn't want someone else to have what I couldn't. The jealousy and bitterness consumed me, and I wanted to see both Camilla and Ben hurt. After they got married, my emotions spiralled even more, and I decided to put a plan in motion to get rid of Ben."

"So, what exactly did your plan to get rid of Ben involve? And did you honestly believe that by doing so, Camilla would come back to you?"

"No, I never truly thought she'd come back. Camilla's a good person—strong and not the type to let others push her around. I've always known that. But before I explain the plan, let me make one thing clear: I'm taking full responsibility for everything. Anyone else involved, their names and roles, will stay with me. This is on me, and me alone."

"To be honest, Richard, right now I just want to know what happened, and then we can figure things out from there."

"Alright. Well, I looked into hiring a hitman—someone who could make it seem like Ben just disappeared, and that would be the end of it."

"What do you mean 'the end of it'? Did he kill Ben?"

"After I hired him and paid him 250,000 pounds in cash, we agreed that he wouldn't tell me what he planned to do with Ben or where he would end up. The idea was that the less I knew, the less chance I'd slip up or face any pressure. My only instruction was to make Ben disappear—permanently—and that was it. But then I heard he'd been found, and according to the news, it had been staged to look like a suicide. However, things didn't add up after the autopsy. But that's where it ended for me. I didn't think much more of it. Yes, I orchestrated it, but I wasn't the one who killed him. I left it at that, thinking it wouldn't be much of an issue, at least to some extent."

"When you found out the news, how did you feel? Did you have any remorse?"

"Not really. It had only been a few years since I got kicked out, and I was still in a pretty bad place emotionally. My life was rough and I mostly tried to block it out."

"Was there any impact from the drugs you were taking?"

"Yeah, definitely. I was using a lot of drugs at the time, which made me care less and less. The more I used, the more indifferent I became. It didn't end there; I just kept going."

"What do you mean by 'it didn't end there'?"

"Well, not long after Ben went missing, my parents kicked me out. I asked most of my friends if I could move in with them, but my drug addiction made me a liability, so no one wanted me around. I decided to go to Camilla and Ben's house. With Ben gone, I thought maybe this was my chance. I figured if I asked to move in and she said yes, it would be a win for me—even though it wasn't really about wanting her. So, I went to their door, offered my condolences with some shortbread, and asked if I could move in because I'd been kicked out. Seb, the estate manager, turned me away. I was furious—probably angrier than ever. Whether the drugs contributed to that, I'm not sure."

"And what did you do with that anger?"

"It drove me to hatch my next plan. After being turned away, I decided to target Camilla's mother. I knew she was staying there temporarily and was set to leave on Wednesday morning. I made arrangements to find out her departure details. I arranged for a 'taxi' to turn up before her scheduled one, making it seem like a mix-up with two taxis arriving. I paid a new contact to handle it—someone more capable of making things happen—and convince her mother to write a letter saying she was unwell and had planned to tell Camilla when she was staying but couldn't bring herself to because of Ben's disappearance."

"When you say 'letter' what was in it?"

"I'm not entirely sure of the details, but somehow, he got Caroline to write a letter explaining she was very sick and might not have long to live. It said that by the time Camilla found it, her mother would likely be dead—something like that. The letter was placed in the house a few days after Caroline left. There was also a phone call, arranged to come from her mother's hospital, from someone pretending to be from the bereavement team, telling Camilla her mother had passed away."

"But how on earth did the letter get into the house?"

"The person who handled it managed to slip it inside. He nearly got caught, though—there's something about that house, with its creaky floors and all. Camilla thought she heard Seb and started shouting for him. Luckily, he got out unseen. It wasn't investigated, though, since as far as I know, Camilla never noticed anything out of place."

"And how did he get past Terry and avoid being seen on CCTV?"

"The grounds aren't fully covered, as you've probably realised during your investigations. You can get into the gardens without being seen. I guess the CCTV was never checked because nothing was ever brought to anyone's attention to warrant it. It was a very close call, though."

"Ok... And is this another case where you're kept in the dark, with no idea what they've done with the body?"

"Not exactly. This time, because I was working with someone different, I chose to be more involved. For instance, I knew her mother's bedsheets were dropped off for dry cleaning—I even dropped Karin off at the cleaners myself. I paid the owner later, asking him to tell Karin that the sheets had gotten mixed up and couldn't be located. She'd be left wondering where they went, with no clue of their real use."

"But why the owl bedspread? Why go through all the trouble of taking it just to use it to hide the body?"

"Karin told me it was special. I had told the guy I hired that I wanted to make Camilla suffer, that I wanted to mess with her in any way I could. Using her mother's bedspread felt like a twisted touch, a way to disturb her if the body were ever found. The man I worked with this time was smart— worth the 500,000 pounds— and a lot more capable than the person I had for Ben."

"What made you think of the well?"

"Well, when he asked me where to dispose of the body, I remembered a hidden well on the estate. Ben and I used to play there as kids, back when it was still visible. I went onto the grounds one night, where I knew there were no cameras, to see if I could find it. It took some effort—it was long overgrown and very well hidden, making it the perfect spot. We dropped the body down, figuring it would take a long time to be discovered, if it ever was. To be sure, the guy even climbed down himself to wedge the body deep into a crevice, making it nearly impossible to discover."

"What steps did you take to ensure everyone believed the death was real?"

"I knew her mother came from a poor family and didn't have much. She'd been sick before, and Ben and Camilla had paid for everything—her house, living expenses—so everything was in their names. There wasn't anything tied directly to her mother that needed closing. That part was easy. The real challenge was getting a doctor to forge a death certificate. I found one who, for a couple of million, was willing to do it. He forged the paperwork, I paid him cash, and it all went smoothly. Then I had a set of ashes sent to Camilla's house, claiming they were her mother's. But they weren't—they were just random ashes from a bonfire. That was the final step. After that, everything fell into place."

"But how did you know so much about her mother's life?"

"Well, that's what I hired someone for. They did all the digging, gathered the details, and gave me everything I needed to know. It wasn't hard to piece it together from there."

"What made you confess to all this now, after over a decade?"

"Because, honestly, I've got nothing left. I'm homeless, living on the streets, and my life is a wreck. I've lost everything, and it feels like I'm already dead. At least if I confess, prison might offer me some sense of stability. I'd have a roof over my head, food to eat, and maybe, just maybe, some peace. It's sad to say, but it feels like prison could give me a better life than the one I have now."

"Alright, Richard, I believe that's enough for today. I've gathered most of the information I need for now. There will be several more interviews to follow, but in the meantime, you'll remain in custody and await further proceedings."

Chapter Twenty-Eight

It took over a year for investigators to piece everything together and carefully construct the evidence that would finally bring Richard to justice. Even after his confession, Richard refused to reveal any names, companies, or details that would implicate the others involved in the crimes. He was adamant on taking the full weight of responsibility on himself, shielding anyone else from facing the same fate. Whether it was out of misplaced loyalty or a desperate bid to maintain some semblance of control, no one could be sure. But one thing was clear: Richard would go down alone.

The trial was a spectacle that gripped the entire nation. What began as whispers of unsolved tragedies spiralled into a shocking revelation of deceit, betrayal, and murder. The courtroom was packed with spectators and journalists eager to witness the downfall of a man who had hidden so much darkness for such a long time. The final verdict—life imprisonment without the possibility of parole—came as a devastating blow to those who had hoped for a different ending. But the burden of Richard's actions, the pain he inflicted, was too much for mercy.

For Camilla, the news was shattering. She had lost her husband and her mother in a way no one should have to endure. As the horrific details unfolded, the world watched her break, her heart clearly torn apart by the revelations. The thought of what her family had suffered in those final days was unbearable. She would carry that burden for the rest of her life—a wound that would never heal.

Richard, once filled with a twisted hope that his confession might bring some kind of redemption, slowly realised that the reality of prison was far worse than he had imagined. He had thought, perhaps naively, that his parents would visit him, that they would offer him some comfort despite the horror of what he had done. But they never came. Week after week passed, and Richard remained alone. He had become a pariah, completely cut off from the people he once knew.

Eventually, it dawned on him: no one would ever visit. His parents, old friends—everyone had turned their backs on him. He would spend the rest of his days in a cell, a forgotten man, living in the shadow of his own monstrous actions. He would die in that prison, unloved and unwanted, a man who had traded everything for a moment of control, only to lose it all.

In the end, Richard wasn't just serving a life sentence in prison. He was serving a life sentence of isolation, knowing he had destroyed not only the lives of those around him but his own soul as well. The world had moved on, and he had been left behind to rot, a grim reminder of the price one pays for unforgivable acts.

Meanwhile, Camilla carved out a new existence for

herself, slowly shedding the stigma that had once clung to her like a shadow. With the local community finally recognising that she was not complicit in Richard's crimes, they began to welcome her back into their midst. Her resilience resonated with those around her, and she found solace in the support of neighbours who had once shunned her. Though she still lived at Middlemoor, the echoes of the past remained in every corner of the estate. She often felt the strain of memories that were too heavy to bear, reminding her of the mayhem that had unfolded. Yet she chose to stay, determined to transform the space into a sanctuary of healing.

With David and the twins by her side, along with the dedicated staff at Middlemoor, Camilla felt a newfound strength. Together, they formed an unwavering support network, each member bolstering the other in times of need. They shared laughter and tears, helping one another heal and rebuild. As they worked side by side on community projects and initiatives, Camilla found joy in the connections they forged, proving that even in the aftermath of tragedy, bonds could be formed that would last a lifetime.

As she stood in the garden one crisp afternoon, watching the sunlight filter through the leaves, Camilla realised that she had finally started to reclaim her life. The comfort of friendship and the strength of community enveloped her, bringing a sense of peace that had long felt elusive. While Richard languished in his prison of despair, she was free: free to dream, free to hope, and free to love again. Surrounded by her army of support, she felt ready to embrace whatever the future held, a testament to the resilience of the human spirit.

And with that realisation, Camilla knew this was not just the end of a chapter, but the beginning of a new story, one filled with promise, healing, and the unwavering belief that brighter days were ahead.

Let's get this estate turned into a wedding venue, Camilla thought to herself, a spark of excitement igniting. She could almost picture it: the grand hall adorned with flowers, the gardens filled with laughter and music, the rooms alive with guests celebrating new beginnings.

But as she wandered back into the house, her mind began to race with questions. Could she really transform Middlemoor into a place of joy and celebration? Would the estate's dark history ever fully release its grip, or would its history always loom over her plans, refusing to fade? What if this was only the beginning...

Acknowledgements

I'd like to take a moment to express my deepest gratitude to someone who has profoundly impacted my life: my former English teacher, Miss Madan, who taught me in sixth form. When I was in secondary school, I struggled with English and unfortunately didn't pass the subject. As a result, it became mandatory for me to retake it in the sixth form.

At that point, I had lost confidence in my abilities and was unsure if I could ever succeed in a subject that had always seemed out of reach for me. But Miss Madan saw something in me that I couldn't see in myself. She believed in my potential even when I didn't.

Thanks to her dedication and belief in my capabilities, I not only passed English but also found a sense of confidence. This newfound confidence has been a driving force behind one of my greatest achievements: writing and publishing my own book.

Miss Madan's faith in me wasn't just about helping me pass an exam—it was about inspiring me to push beyond my limits and pursue my dreams. Her influence has extended far beyond the classroom and has had a lasting impact on my life. I know that I'm not alone in this; many of her students deeply value her for the profound ways she has shaped our lives and futures. For that, I am incredibly grateful. Thank you, Miss Madan, for being the guiding light that helped me—and so many others—find our paths.

Printed in Dunstable, United Kingdom